Baking and Blindfolds

A Stepbrother Reverse Harem Romance

Baking and Blindfolds

A Stepbrother Reverse Harem Romance

Part of the

Christmas Cherry Auction series

Sylvie Haas

Copyright

Contents

Blurb   VIII

1. One   1
   Bianca

2. Two   10
   Mark

3. Three   14
   Carl

4. Four   18
   Sean

5. Five   22
   Bianca

6. Six   30
   Sean

7. Seven   34
   Bianca

8. Eight   38
    Carl

9. Nine   42
    Bianca

10. Ten   48
    Carl

11. Eleven   53
    Bianca

12. Twelve   61
    Sean

13. Thirteen   67
    Bianca

14. Fourteen   72
    Carl

15. Fifteen   75
    Mark

16. Sixteen   79
    Bianca

17. Seventeen   88
    Carl

18. Eighteen   91
    Bianca

19. Nineteen   94
    Mark

20. Twenty   103
    Sean

21. Epilogue   111
    Carl

22. More from Sylvie Haas   116

23. Sylvie Haas Freebies   118

24. About the Author   119

Blurb

Cooking with my stepbrothers really heats things up.

I'm a disappointment.

A failure.

A burden.

That's how my billionaire father and his wife see me.

After getting dumped and flunking out of college, there's only one place left to go: back home. The last thing I want is to see that look of utter disgust in my father's eyes and that smug smirk on my stepmother's face, yet again. But the one thing I do want is to get over my ex and finally take control of my own life.

And I know exactly the man--or men--for the job. Getting my stepbrothers to bid on me in the Christmas Cherry Auction should get the ball rolling. It's time to make their resistance waiver. Torn between their desire to please me in every way possible and their loyalty to my father's wallet for their up and coming business proposal, it's going to take a Christmas miracle to get the gift that I really want this season.

And I know it's the gift that will keep on giving!

If you love dirty-talking men who know how to please their stepsister, don't miss this year's Christmas Cherry Auction!

One

Bianca

Chimes ring from my phone, alerting me that the first twenty minutes of sunbathing are over. I tap the Restart button and sit up to flip onto my stomach, but stop midway and carefully set my oversized, cat-eye sunglasses with cute rhinestones at the tips on my stepmom's teak side table.

I'm more worried about scratching her precious table than ruining my glasses. I don't have the funds to replace either.

Cranking the space heater up, I sip my celebratory sparkling cider and take in the penthouse balcony view of the mountains. The snow-capped peaks mimic the puffy clouds set against the crystal blue sky. Sunbathing in December may not be my brightest idea, but I'm determined to stand on stage at tonight's auction with bright sun-kissed cheeks.

Both sets.

Hopefully, my stepbrothers find out about the second set tonight.

Bottoms up for the next twenty minutes, then a long, warm, bubbly soaker bath before my deep dive beauty prep for tonight's auction at the sex club.

The freshman fifteen makes me slightly conscious of my belly as I settle in to sun my buns. I tug the bottom of my suit into my crack for better exposure and unhook my top. The warmth of the sun on my body is pure joy.

Can I be as lucky as the women who participated in last year's auction? They all ended up in reverse harem relationships with billionaires. One of the women weighs heavily on my mind since her stepbrothers bought her.

Will my stepbrothers accept the anonymous invitation I sent? Technically the auction isn't for a relationship or even sex, but fantasies are king...and I'm their queen.

In reality, my world is falling apart. Or maybe it fell apart and is drumming its fingers on the table, like everyone else, waiting for me to quit being a disappointment and figure out how to put my life back together.

Loud voices and the crash of one wooden chair into another startle me from the next balcony.

"You'd be a fucking moron to think I'd do that, Sean," my stepbrother Mark yells at one of my other two stepbrothers. All three of them live in the other penthouse. I imagine Mark shoving his long bangs to the side so the full extent of his ire can beam from his eyes.

My arm extends reflexively, my fingers tangling in my robe. There's no actual worry about being seen, there's a solid divider between the two balconies.

I'd welcome one of my fantasies playing out. My brothers would peek around the edge of the balcony and catch me—

Now isn't the time. The garbled words I think I hear from inside their apartment have my full attention... 'the invitation' and 'tonight'.

Did they figure out I'm in the auction? Is going to the auction the thing Mark would have to be a moron to do? Are they disgusted at the thought of bidding on me?

Me. Their emotional little stepsister who let a bad breakup derail her college classes. The immature girl who had to move in with the stepmom she despises. The pathetic sister who took a job as Santa's helper because they were willing to hire me on the spot.

This is the exact opposite of how I imagined tonight going.

Unable to make out the words of the brother who's still inside their penthouse, I let go of my robe, stand up, refasten my top, and tug the bottom of my bathing suit to a less invasive position.

With my ear pressed to the divider between the balconies, I strain to hear.

"You're just an asshole," Mark, the brother on the balcony says. Surely he's not this upset at Sean. Aside from Sean's friends-with-everyone nature, his baby face adds to his friendly demeanor.

Ugh! What did I miss? Is it time to abandon my stealth efforts and let them know I'm the one who sent the invitation? I bite my lower lip.

I don't want them to bid on me out of pity. It's not like I'd even benefit from the money since it goes to charity. I might actually have to donate four hours of my time to help the winner prepare for the holidays.

It's a far cry from feeling desirable. I want to be loved. I want my stepbrothers. They'd be a safe way to lose my virginity.

More realistically, I want the fantasy. Saying something now could bring it crashing down. Silence is my best bet.

Their argument continues. "How bad would it piss off Frank?" That must be my confirmation that they know I'm in the auction. Carl's the pensive brother, always crafting strategies, but what does he have against my dad?

"How long do you think it would take for rumors to surface?" Sean is in on the ulterior motives?

Is it too late to back out? Aurora and Cindy would kill me, but as I'm surrounded by luxury, I shouldn't bite the hand that feeds me. I grab my phone and send a group text to my girlfriends: *Might not make it tonight*

"I'm not sure what would be more priceless, if we all bought her or..." Sean's voice fades.

It's a game to them. An evil plot. I'm crushed.

I stare at my phone. Why haven't my girls texted back?

"I'm heading to the bar," Marks says. Their door slams.

My stomach sinks. It's lose-lose. My grand plan that my brothers bid on me can't happen if they spend their normal Friday night with friends. But if they show up, there will be collateral damage.

Fantasy might not have been king when it comes to them.

Or perhaps queen was the overstatement. Court jester? Family fuck up? The first college dropout?

I try to focus on the positive...nope. My splurge on the adorable Santa's helper costume and black knee-high boots that have white fur around the top is a waste.

I've practiced strutting in my boots so the soles are bound to show wear. I can't return them.

"Are you snooping on your stepbrothers?" The nasal accusation of my stepmom's voice smacks me from behind as her too-much floral scent invades my nose.

Gripping one hand on the rail and using the other to comb through my hair, I stand taller and turn. Her bright magenta suit is as potent as her perfume.

"No. Why would I do that?" The elevated pitch of my voice and the way the words spew from my mouth betray me.

"I could ask that of most things about you. Like why you threw college away just because your boyfriend found someone new. It's quite—"

"I didn't throw college away."

"Two F's, a D—"

"Stop." Pinching the bridge of my nose, I take a deep breath.

"How do you plan on taking care of yourself without a college degree?"

"I'm filling out applications. I'll find somewhere to go." Vulnerability eats at me as her eyes rake up and down my body. I cross my arms and look at the mountains.

"Now, to earn your keep, I need you to pick up the invitations for my gala." She hands me a business card I hadn't noticed she was holding. "They're open for one more hour, and the guest list is on your desk. They need to be delivered to the post office tomorrow at the latest."

I laugh.

That was the wrong thing to do. She's serious.

"It's hardly funny that the printer forgot to emboss the filigree on the envelopes. Their delay puts me perilously close to only getting the invitations out two months in advance."

I laugh again, although it's actually a scoff of disbelief if I was forced to categorize the sound.

Her scowl indicates it's still the wrong thing to do.

"The post office closes at two on Saturday," I say, as if she cares about mortal constraints.

"I suppose you can't sleep until two then."

Tension in my jaw has to be nearing teeth-shattering levels.

No matter how much I despise my stepmom, I appreciate that she's the one who convinced my dad to let me stay here.

I don't know if he agreed, but he's out of the country so there wasn't much he could do.

My real mom, who I always lived with, just moved in with a guy. She says it's too early in the relationship for me to complicate things by moving in, which basically means I've become her baggage.

So, my stepmom's offer of penthouse living, where she might consider me her personal assistant, won out over being homeless.

"I have plans tonight. Would it be okay if I get the invitations in the mail on Monday?"

Her eyes pause on my belly. "Now isn't the time to be slack about commitments and let yourself go."

I relent, to avoid a lecture. "Let me get dressed. I can pick them up and still go out with my friends. I'll tackle the addresses in the morning."

"There are exactly one thousand invitations. Make sure your handwriting stays pretty."

Crap.

Turning off the space heater, I grab my belongings and stifle my desire to stomp to my room. It would only give her one more reason to chastise me.

Signing up for the Christmas Cherry Auction was a dumb idea. My father's right. I'm too lost in daydreams like my mom. I might as well have plucked petals from a flower to ask the universe if my stepbrothers could love me.

Aurora and Cindy's messages finally come in and offer another perspective. I have to attend...or they'll kill me.

But Aurora's last message hits another sore spot. My ex. *Don't let Damon get the best of you. Put on your big girl thong and be outside your building on time.*

I wish he was the problem.

I don't want to be the pawn in some rude game my brothers are playing.

Me: *My stepbrothers want to irritate my dad by bidding on me.*

Aurora: *WTF?*

Cindy: *They're idiots. Let's beat them at their own game.*

Me: *How*

Cindy: *We'll run their bid up and all they'll get is four hours of holiday prep help, exactly as you signed up to do. Your dad can be proud that so much money will go to charity.*

She has a point. I can stay in charge. They'll have nothing on me, which means... The least I can do is fulfill my responsibility.

The musky scents of my stepbrothers' colognes linger in the elevator when I enter.

Swoony fantasies about elevator sex—

No. My stepbrothers are a great starting place for this new leaf I'm turning over. No more fantasies. Watch out world, Bianca's embracing a new reality.

I don't have a thing for my stepbrothers.

I don't, not anymore

8

I stop squeezing my thighs together.

Time to move on...as soon as the elevator stops spinning.

Two

Mark

"Try flipping the script," Sean says.

"Try driving with your mouth shut." I'm thankful I can see the bar. I need a drink before I blow a gasket. Bianca occupies all of my thoughts. She makes me tingly...and I'm not a tingly kind of guy. She makes me think of houses with white-picket fences and other things that don't fit into my jet-set lifestyle.

How can I want her so badly when she's exactly what I don't want? Mom had a streak of disastrous relationships before meeting Bianca's dad. I don't ever want to hurt a woman the way men hurt her.

"Instead of you pulling Bianca out of the auction, what if we let it go on as planned and I win her?"

"You won't because I told you not to." I can't deal with the thought of what he wants to do with her. His intent can't be far from my own, which I can barely tamp down. And if either of us screws our stepsister, we stand to complicate our family and business in one harsh blow.

"Let's say I got the high bid. I could fund the entire goal for the women's shelter."

"No."

"Why not? You want to be the shining star? You want to control what Bianca does with the four hours of her volunteer time?"

"Bianca's not taking part in the auction."

"What if you don't get to decide what she does with her life?"

"I'm not letting our eighteen-year-old, as in she's legally an adult, stepsister sell herself."

"Don't patronize me."

"Don't interfere with my plan."

Sean's exasperated sigh as he turns into the parking lot amps up my need for alcohol.

"The only part of your plan I agree with is that we get some drinks in you so you can calm down, hopefully not make a fool of yourself."

"What about Bianca making a fool of *her*self, or of our family? Have you thought about that?" I slam my door and beeline for the bar.

The rush of Sean hurrying over the gravel lot and his continued pleadings don't help any. "Trust me. I've thought about her walking across that stage and what she thinks will happen."

My cock thickens as he forces the thought into my mind. "We have to think of what's best for the family."

"You're assuming she wants the same thing we do. She's not like us."

The bartender nods as we enter. I hold up two fingers, and he gets to work on my usual.

"She loves luxury as much as the rest of us. She'll need a career." The ease with which lies flow from my tongue should bother me. What I really want is to lock Bianca in the highest room of the tallest tower and keep her for myself. She wouldn't need a career. She'd need me and only me. But I've seen how relationships change men, ruin their drive for success. Then they start a family and become domesticated.

I'm not ready to be tied down. And her father's been a generous mentor when he's not busy being a prick.

"Everyone loves luxury, but all she talks about in her future is a family. You ever notice she doesn't mention a career or lavish trips?"

"That doesn't mean she doesn't want them."

"But it means that when she looks at her future, there are things more important than professional success."

The bartender brings me two Rusty Nails. They'll either calm me down or they'll seal my coffin when I make a scene at the auction.

I can't stand the thought of anyone, even my brothers, buying Bianca. Even if it is for four innocent hours, I'd lose my fucking mind. Which means there's only one solution. If I can't get her out of the auction, I have to win the bid.

That's a dangerous path. If I buy her, I'm responsible for her. A lot can happen in four hours. But I'm not the settling-down kind of guy she wants. I've crafted my entire career around never being limited to one location. A fucking catch-22.

Three

Carl

Sean and I decided that he should go with Mark to the bar. It's a chance for Sean to figure out what has Mark so riled.

I suspect he's as obsessed with Bianca as I am, but we've never spoken about beyond-sisterly feelings, or how we'd deal with one of us dating her.

My ulterior motive was to go straight to the auction and make a game plan to try to keep Mark from turning this evening into a fiasco and embarrassing Bianca.

The last few days since she's been back in town have unlocked my creative genius. I've had more breakthroughs for work projects and an idea for a special feature to add to our app.

I've never been the type to credit a muse for my inspiration but when I think of her, the world comes alive.

I can't let Mark fuck this up. I need Bianca in ways I've denied. And from what I've heard, her boyfriend broke up with her. That shouldn't be a green flag for me, but fuck if I don't want to help ease her through the heartbreak.

The doors to the sex club are locked. The bodyguard outside shakes his head when I try the handle, even though he told me that I couldn't go in yet.

He glances at his watch. "Five more minutes."

I note his name embroidered on his barely-big-enough black polo. "It's an emergency, Winger."

"What kind of emergency?"

"I have to talk to my stepsister. It's a private matter."

"Is her life in danger?"

"No."

"Is there a death in the family?"

"No." Although I seriously wonder if somebody's life might be in danger if they bid on her. That's not likely to carry any weight with Winger.

Five minutes pass and I expect the door to open from the inside, but to my surprise, Winger pulls keys from his pocket and unlocks the doors. I decide not to voice my thoughts that he's a dick for making me wait.

As I make my way through the club, I ask the wait staff where the women for auction are and get mixed answers anywhere from no one's allowed in with them to waitresses pointing in the general direction of the stage.

I head for the door beside the stage where a bodyguard with a similarly strained polo to the guy outside, although this one named Mammoth, steps in front of me.

"I have to talk to Bianca." I point as if I know where she is.

"The only talking they want to hear tonight is the auctioneer rattling numbers each time you raise your paddle."

"She's my stepsister."

Mammoth smirks.

"It's not like that." Except it is. That crazy inspiration I get from Bianca is unlike anything I've ever experienced. Probably the taboo nature. Stepsisters shouldn't have such long legs, tiny waist, and plump tits. She's a hummingbird in a family of vultures. She's a relief.

I have to shake the thought of settling down with her from my mind. Monotony stifles creativity.

"Sign-up is over there." Mammoth extends his tree-trunk sized arm.

I follow the direction he indicates and get that out of the way in case it's necessary. Then I stake out the front table since others are filing in.

I pat the bidding number against my thigh, lift it, and imagine I'm the winning bid. Exhilaration shoots through me. My cock swells before I get control.

I can't imagine what her dad would think. The charitable donation defense would go over better than the truth of making sure no one got their hands on her because she's mine. It's very clear in my mind how this needs to work.

Mammoth walks past. I pop up once he safely has his back to me and I head for the side door.

"Do not touch that handle," he booms.

"Look dude, it's my sister. I need to talk to her."

"What's your name?"

"Carl."

"Your message?" His crossed arms indicate he doesn't give a fuck what my message is.

"It's personal. Just tell her I need to talk to her."

He vanishes, then comes back and shakes his head. "The lady said no."

Four

Sean

Mark opens the car door and hurls himself toward the entry of the Aubergine Affair sex club when I've barely stopped the vehicle. Two Rusty Nails were not enough to take the edge off.

I jump out of the car, circle around, and barely catch up with him by the time he's made his way inside to the tables directly in front of the stage where Carl is sitting.

Mark growls, "What the fuck is that?"

Carl gives a half smile and flashes the bidding paddle as he stands. "In case we have to bid."

"Do not bid on Bianca."

"It's one way to get her out of here." The undertones of Carl's excitement confirm that she's gotten to all of us.

"If anyone's going to bid on her, it's me." Mark seems to think he gets to call the shots. He's the oldest, but that hasn't mattered for a long time.

"That's up for discussion," Carl says.

Mark reaches for the paddle, but Carl jerks it back throwing his other hand against our brother's chest. "Get your own damn number."

"Or we can go in together as one big happy family," I reason.

"Then we're doing it under my number." The corded muscles in Mark's neck flex.

Why the hell does he choose to be agreeable now? I regret my suggestion. Keeping the peace is usually my priority but I won't pass up a chance to officially win Bianca, to lay claim to her. There's something about her that all the other women I've dated don't have.

I change my approach. "Or we can bid against each other and drive the price up. It's all about charity, right?" I give them a wink and walk off to register.

Mark follows me, grumbling the whole time, then we meet back at the table.

"So...what would you do with Bianca for four hours?" Is anyone ready to admit what's haunting each of us. The silence shuts that conversation down.

"We've got to get her out before this shit storm starts." Mark is barely calmer than before.

"It's only going to be a shit storm if you make it one," Carl says.

Mark charges off and is met by a bodyguard who refuses to let him in the back. As Mark seems to be returning to our seats, he puts a hand on the edge of the stage and I think he's going to jump up, but the bodyguard jumps up faster and towers over him. "Do you need to be escorted out of here?"

I cringe internally, wondering if the first wave of the storm has hit. Nobody gets away with talking to Mark like that.

I'm shocked when Mark lifts his hands. "Have it your way."

He returns to the table. "I'll do the bidding and handle her afterward."

If I'd drawn a line in the sand, Mark just crossed it. "She's not a piece of property to be handled."

"She put herself in an auction. Are you oblivious to what these men would do with her?"

"It's not just about protecting her from other bidders. I want more than four hours of her time." Did I just pull the pin on a hand grenade? My heart's about to explode. My brothers and I have come to blows on a few occasions. If I wasn't cool-natured, it would happen more often, but this time I'm the antagonist.

Mark says, "She's our step-sister."

Carl stumbles on a few words before he finally says, "You want a relationship with her? Have you thought about how it would affect Mark and me?"

The jealousy in his words betrays the simple questions.

My phone buzzes. After a glance I dismiss it.

Carl asks, "One of your girlfriends?"

"Fuck you."

"That's what she wants." Mark makes a lame joke but he's not wrong.

"It's just a friend."

"A female one?"

"I'm capable of having female friends."

"Enough that you don't need to add Bianca to the list." Carl won't be swayed easily.

"She wouldn't just be added to a list. I want to explore things with her."

Mark might be experiencing an aneurysm, but until he drops to the ground, I'll assume he's okay.

Carl says, "A few hours ago you didn't even know she was in the auction. You're going from zero to fucking her awfully fast."

Mark growls, "Not a chance."

I've confessed my feelings. I'm in now. I have to win this. "Give me one good reason I can't date her, aside from she's our stepsister."

Mark slams his fist on the table. "She has dreams we can't fulfill. Besides her father would pull his investment if we gang banged his princess."

Did he just admit his feelings? "We?"

Five

Bianca

"Not a chance." The deep, gravelly voice carries onto the wings of the stage where my friends and I are waiting. Unmistakably a pissed off Mark.

So, all three of my brothers probably came since the bodyguard let me know Carl was here. I declined to talk since I didn't want anything to mess up my chance to participate in the auction. If they think it's disgusting, that's their problem, not mine.

Could I be happy with a different set of billionaires? It's like being in the mood for a triple-chocolate brownie and being offered a cherry lollipop.

I pull the velvet curtain to the side a couple of inches to find my brothers and see why Mark is yelling. It's not unlike him.

He's now in a seat at one of the front tables, a bodyguard standing interestingly close to him.

Mark leans forward, head bowed, his forearms on his knees, a bidder's paddle clutched in his hand. Carl and Sean have paddles too.

Hmmm... in my fantasy, they're a package deal. How would it work with just one of them? Such a problem would be a blessing.

I wiggle as veins of excitement shoot through me. The bodyguard steps away. If Mark's anger was dialed up anymore, he might just burst into white-hot flames. Not good.

The other brothers wear strained expressions but not as intensely as Mark.

My attention is drawn to motion as he rises. Our eyes lock as he unfolds himself from the chair and strides toward the stage.

My pulse pounds in my ears.

The bodyguard catches his arm and steps in front of him. The two men square off. This could go wrong. Should I swallow my pride and intervene?

I close the curtain and turn to Aurora and Cindy, hoping they'll offer good advice.

"I shouldn't be here. That argument I heard with my brothers earlier, I'm messing everything up."

"No, you can't leave. You've been so excited about this." Aurora and her cheery demeanor can barely break through my nerves. The announcer's voice booms over the PA system, rattling me to the core.

"You have to go," Cindy says. "You're first."

The key issue here is that if I don't go first, Cindy will be. She was clear that she didn't want to be first or last. She wanted to be sandwiched safely in the middle.

"I don't think I can go through with it. Mark's going to cause a scene. If I just leave, we can pretend like none of this ever happened."

"Think of the women's shelter," Aurora says.

"I'm sure you two will raise enough."

"And you don't want to be a part of that?"

She knows how to get at me. My stepmom is really big on fundraising, and I'm trying to be more of an adult and emulate her selfless actions. Even though, for the most part, I could never be like her. But that's one thing she gets right.

The door slams and adrenaline spikes through me that it's Mark. It's not.

"What are you doing here, Wendy? Aren't you getting married today?"

We're not close friends and I heard it was going to be a small ceremony. Who knows, I might have gotten the date wrong. She's in sweats so that's no help. But her frantic expression hints that she might have bigger problems than I do.

As she wrings her hands and takes a few deep breaths, I note what Jefferson, the emcee for the evening, is saying. "Thank you for showing up. Let's make this bigger than last year. In case anyone isn't aware of how this works, the women have agreed to volunteer four hours of their time to help with holiday preparations, nothing more...unless mutually agreed upon."

Wendy's shaky voice pulls me back. "I couldn't do it. I couldn't be a piece of property getting traded as part of a business deal. My dad, my boyfriend...if they don't respect me now, how do I think they ever will? I had to stand up for myself?"

"I had no idea that's why you were getting married." I feel dumbfounded that people still do that.

Aurora hugs her. "You want to be a part of the auction? I couldn't decide between two dresses so I have an extra."

Wendy's voice wavers. "I hate to admit this, but I came here on purpose. I saw the contract. My virginity was part of the deal my father offered to his pervy friend. I want to officially break the contract."

"We can't guarantee who will win you, but remember, you don't have to have sex."

"I know. Thanks, ladies."

Aurora nearly whispers, "Everyone from last year's auction ended up marrying the guys that bought them."

Wendy grimaces. "I doubt I'll be that lucky, but as I ran through the room, I saw quite a few guys I'd be happy to make a deal with."

"Well, last year was an anomaly," Cindy says. "I don't know that we can count on that, but the auction is for a good cause. And well, quite frankly, what better way to lose our V-cards than with experienced guys. I mean, if it all pans out. If not, we just clean a house or wrap presents for four hours."

Aurora pulls us in for a huddle. "It's showtime. They just called Bianca..."

Did they?

Aurora continues, "Cindy is second, and I was going to go last, but you can go before or after me, I don't care."

Jefferson emphasizes my name over the PA. "Let's give a round of applause for Bianca Sinclair."

The roar of the crowd grows. My confidence ticks up one notch. I tug my skirt down.

Aurora slaps my hand. "Enough of that. I know you think you're not pretty enough, not skinny enough, but you're skinnier than all of us. And it wouldn't matter if you weren't. Don't let your stepmom get in your head. Walk out there, chin high, tits out, and let that money roll in."

She slaps my ass then guides me to the edge of the curtain.

As she pulls it back, my eyes land on the front table where my three brothers are still sitting. Mark has gone from irritated to feral. Our eyes lock again and he lifts from his chair, but a slight shift from the bodyguard causes Mark to sit. What the hell did that dude say to him to get him under his finger?

I'm conscious of teetering my way to the center of the stage, breathing a sigh of relief when the auctioneer starts rattling numbers, but then it starts to blur.

My brothers raise their paddles. Other people do too, but it's my brothers. They keep bidding on me. Up and up. I can't understand a word the auctioneer says except for the occasional repeated number.

Then suddenly... "Sold!"

The room spins and I fear that I'll faint. Won't that be disappointing. Thankfully, Jefferson wraps his arm around me. Could he tell? I lean into him.

How did I miss all of the bids? How did I miss the "Going, going, gone"? Was that even said? How much did I go for? Who won me?

"Get off the stage." The low, growly reverb of Mark's voice answers my question. He's getting up from his chair, and the bodyguard doesn't stop Mark from hopping on stage this time.

Chaos erupts from the back of the room. Whoops and hollers, but it can't be about my bid. I pull my eyes from Mark as he stampedes toward me.

It's Aurora's brothers, the rock stars. They have a concert tonight. Why the hell are they here?

I look to the side and catch Aurora staring wide-eyed, then suddenly I'm swooped off my feet.

My hands flail to stop my fall, but strong, thick arms wrap around me, curling me into the contours of Mark's chest. My flail lands my arms around his neck. Our faces are inches apart.

Through the anger, the intensity, I see something more intriguing...desire.

He barks at Carl. "Go wrap up the payment."

As Mark moves furiously toward the exit, his chest rises and falls with heavy breaths. He's even harder than I imagined. Electricity zings through my body. Will it be just him, or all three?

"What the hell were you thinking?"

The sexy stepbrother fantasy bubble bursts.

I'm too embarrassed to answer. I've successfully pissed him off.

I shouldn't be lost in the woody musk of his cologne tinged with alcohol. I should be gathering my senses. All of them, the logical ones included.

Gathering a moment of clarity, I toss out my prefab answer. "It's for charity."

The chill from his demeanor is colder than the winter evening. And the storm in his eyes rages deeper than the front that's supposed to blow in.

He continues to Sean's car but doesn't set me down. "You're half naked. Everyone knows what you're hoping for."

Apparently not, but I don't say anything. I'm saved by Carl and Sean rushing to our sides. Cindy's running out behind them with my bag.

"Why aren't you on stage?"

Sean takes my bag.

"Aurora's brothers demanded they be allowed to buy her right away."

Oh no, Cindy was worried about the order. Low rumbles from the street catch everyone's attention. Motorcycles file into the parking lot.

"Get the fucking car unlocked," Mark demands.

Sean holds the keys up. "Chill, we already paid. No need to scare her."

Sean cups his hand over mine, pulling it from around Mark's neck. "You want him to set you down?"

"Get the fucking car unlocked. I'm not setting her down until I can get her away from the horny-as-fuck rock stars and now this motorcycle gang."

This isn't the way I fantasized he'd want to protect me.

His voice grows louder as he turns, our faces just inches apart.

"Did it not occur to you that the auction was moved to a sex club for a reason?"

Any threads of my fantasy that were hanging on unravel. Is he going to chastise me for the four hours he won? This isn't the kind of tongue-lashing I hoped for.

Six

Sean

The members of the motorcycle club barely glance at Bianca. They're looking for someone and she isn't that person. Their dismissal of her puts Mark at ease enough that I get the car unlocked, the passenger door open, and convince him to put her inside.

He buckles her seatbelt. I rub the back of my neck, waiting to see if he'll go for a kiss. I'm the only one who admitted to wanting her. I'm clearly not alone in my feelings though, and that complicates every fucking thing.

Crisis averted for now as his bulky torso backs away from the car, no kiss.

I say, "Carl, you drive Mark home, that'll give everybody a chance to cool off."

"I don't need time to cool off," Mark says.

"Then why are your fists clenched?"

He furrows his brow and lifts his hands, surprise barely hidden on his face as he flexes his fingers. Mark's voice fails to ease. "It was all falling apart."

"Stop. You're scaring her. Can you see that this is not the look of a woman who's pleased? Do you know what that looks like?"

My phone dings. I glance at the screen.

Mark takes a jab at me. "Is that one of the many women you've pleased?"

In the dim lighting of the parking lot, can he tell that my glare conveys, 'Not in front of Bianca'?

I turn the spotlight back on his asshole behavior. "Nothing's falling apart. You made a giant donation. You're fabulous. You should be happy you won Bianca, and we're taking her back to our place."

Carl huffs. "Come on Mark. You need to chill."

Mark steps toward Carl's car while pointing at me. "Don't try anything. We'll be on your tail."

I slip into the driver's seat and set my hand on Bianca's in a semi-friendly gesture. "He'll calm down. He was just trying to protect you."

"I'm an adult."

"That's the problem." I work my fingers around her palm.

"Can we just drive quietly?" She squeezes my hand.

Why do we fit so well? The backs of my fingers touch her thigh.

My cock shifts into Erection mode, and I have to take my hand off hers so I can shift the car into Reverse then Drive.

True to Carl's word, he stays on my tail.

I resist the urge to reach up and brush her cheek, cup her chin, pull her closer, and plant a kiss on her lips. They'd see that through the back windshield for sure.

We arrive home at the same time and file into the elevator. The silence makes the elevator ride last about an hour longer than normal even with the keycard that takes us directly to the top without stopping at any other floors.

The doors open and Bianca steps to the left towards mom's penthouse.

Carl gently says, "We're over here."

"I'm staying with your mom. I thought you knew."

That's an interesting piece of information Mom forgot to mention.

"Not anymore," Mark says, missing the point that we're trying to be respectful.

Carl is more skilled with his words. "What Conan is trying to say is that we need to talk. Will you come over, please?"

"I get it. I shouldn't have shamed the family." She pulls her hair in front of her cleavage. That should be a sin. The only thing that belongs between her tits is my tongue or my cock.

"You didn't shame anyone." I step closer, but she parries with a step back, a step away from me.

I offer all that I can. "Bianca, we need to talk about what happened and what we all expect or what we all hope will happen now that we won you in the auction."

"I won her," Mark says.

Seven

Bianca

Being locked in Mark's bedroom is the less important half of my fantasy. The key part that he missed was that I wanted him on the same side of the door as me.

If I'd known my brothers had something to sort, I could have gone home.

Their discussion sounds like another argument, but other than raised voices, I can't make anything out.

How could Mark be so mad at me?

I slump onto his bed. His bed—a place I've longed to be, a place I imagined getting tossed onto as he climbed over me. I take off my boots and bring my feet onto the bed, slipping them under the covers, as I sink into the plush mattress, pull the top sheet over me, and nuzzle my head into his downy pillow.

I breathe in the musky scent. It's missing the alcohol from earlier. Is that why he's so upset? The alcohol? I rake my hand over the silky sheets and onto a different fabric. I lift my head, assess that it's a t-shirt, and bring it to my face.

I'm shameless at this point. If they're going to take a minute, so am I. There's one part of my fantasy I can control—having an orgasm in my brother's bed. Fantasy will always be king.

I stare at the door, focusing on their grumblings, making sure they're not approaching, and slide my hand between my legs.

My phone dings. Damn it.

A text from Damon, my ex: *What's up*

His level of stupidity.

Damon again: *Want to hang out?*

Not unless you want to give me an orgasm. I set my phone aside.

Ding.

You've got to be kidding me. Can my evening get any worse?

It's not him this time. Aurora added Wendy to the group chat with Cindy.

Another ding. Aurora: *I'm hidden backstage at my stepbrothers' concert. How is everyone else?*

Me: *LOL. I'm locked in Mark's room, but not in a good way.*

Aurora: *How is that not good?*

Me: *I have time to text you, which means I'm not busy with them. They're arguing about something.*

Aurora: *(hug emoji)*

Me: *I can't believe your stepbrothers showed up. Were our expectations too high?*

35

Aurora: *I never thought I'd have a chance with my brothers in a million years but I'm downing some liquid courage since they bought me*

Me: *I'll cross my fingers for you to get to uncross your legs! (wink emoji) (eggplant emoji)*

Aurora: *same*

At least one of us has a chance. I type back: *They'll have to let me out by morning so I can address their mom's invites. Or if they take too long, I can text her and tell her they're keeping me from doing it. Stepmom to the rescue.*

Aurora: *Want me to help with the invites?*

Me: *Sure*

Aurora: *We can swap stories*

Me: *Not the story I was hoping for*

Aurora: *count on our damn brothers to screw things up*

I time myself 'pretend' addressing an envelope then use my phone calculator to determine how long it will take to do that times a thousand. Aurora and I agree on a time to meet.

I drop the phone and remember I'm in Mark's bed...alone. It's amazing how many things I can fail at.

Sliding my hand between my legs, I press gently. I've been so wound up all evening, it takes nothing for the swirl of an orgasm to start building. I grab a pillow and put it on my chest. It's not heavy enough to be one of my brothers, but it's better than nothing.

The bedroom door flies open.

"You should have knocked!" The first part of my statement comes out as more of a pant but I'm screaming by the end as I scramble to sit.

I stare at the three of them huddled in the doorway. Do they realize they barged in on a private moment?

Would it change their reaction if they did? I'm pretty sure I can't stoop any lower. Being at a low point is oddly liberating.

For a moment, I savor the way they're staring at me—like they want me.

Eight

Carl

Bianca's moan and what seemed to be her hand between her legs stymy me. Did we walk in on her... No. Surely she wouldn't... My muse is a naughty one, perhaps Erato or Thalia. Why the hell am I pondering Greek Muses when mine is right here?

"Unless you boys have plans for me, I have to get home. Your mom needs me." The taunt in her tone hints at a sassier side I'm not used to.

Her fingers toy with the edge of the sheet as if waiting for us to call her bluff.

I'm quick to say, "We're not done. We need you—"

Mark cuts me off. "To explain why you were in that auction."

Damn him. Is he completely unable to pivot? Walking in on her hand between her legs should have moved us past the question we agreed he could ask first.

Sean's phone buzzes. He ignores it.

"I already explained—to raise money for the women's shelter."

"Why were you dressed like that?" Mark doesn't relent.

She tosses the covers back, and for a fleeting second, I'm expecting to see her perfect tits, to find out how rosy or dusky her nipples are. But it's all red and white fabric. The only things she's taken off are her boots.

Sean's phone buzzes again.

Bianca pauses but Sean waves a dismissive hand. She answers Mark's question with a light tone. "Some of us are in a festive, *giving* mood."

"Giving?" I step into the room. Mark follows and Sean stops on the other side of him.

She rolls onto her side and throws her legs over the edge of the bed as she sits.

Sean's phone buzzes yet again.

"See what your damn girlfriends need," Mark says.

"I don't have a girlfriend." Sean pulls his phone from his pocket and swipes messages from the screen. "It's nobody important."

Bianca's phone buzzes.

Relief washes over Sean's expression. "See. I'm not the only one who gets texts."

Mark raises an eyebrow at Bianca. She grabs her phone and flusters before poking at the screen several times and setting it aside. If she always pokes it that hard, I might understand why the screen is so cracked.

"Who was that?" Mark asks.

"My ex. It's no big deal. We've all been in other relationships."

Sean rubs a hand over his face, and Mark asks, "What does he want?"

"The question should be what I want."

"Okay. What do you want?"

"He dumped me, and I want to get over him. That's why I was at the auction tonight, other than charity, of course." Bianca's response shuts Mark down.

Sean says, "Looks like I'm not the only one ready to move on. Get over your ex how?"

She grabs her shoes and pushes off the bed, walking toward us. The come hither look I swear she's giving us is replaced by an eye roll.

Sean, usually the gentlest of the three of us, grabs her arm. "How can we help?"

She pulls away and slumps with a heavy exhale. "I can't believe I have to spell this out to my older brothers."

Words fall from my mouth before I can stop them. "Were you hoping to get laid?"

Mark, being ever so not helpful in this conversation, says, "No."

Bianca laughs as Sean and I simultaneously say, "Shut up, Mark."

"Don't fucking tell me what to do." He pushes the two of us aside, steps toward Bianca, cups her chin, turns her face upward, and lands his lips on hers.

When he finally pulls away, he says, "Did that help?"

Nine

Bianca

Mark's words meet my ears, which means he can't be kissing me anymore. The pressure of his lips lingers on mine. I lift a hand in disbelief, covering my lips before I force my eyes open.

Shoot. I must look like an idiot. I clear my throat and move my hand to my hair, pretending to straighten it.

That kiss did a lot more than make me forget about my ex. I forgot how to speak.

Everyone's staring at me. Am I going through with this?

Mark grumbles something then barges past his brothers. The door to their penthouse slams a few seconds later.

I wait. There's no other sound.

He's gone.

How on earth did I screw that up? I stare at my feet, curious how my previous low point has been surpassed. If Carl and Sean hadn't closed the space in front of me, I'd rush out too.

Forcing my chin up, I let my eyes move from Mark's picture of the Colosseum to the Eiffel Tower and Stonehenge and several other noteworthy landmarks. It's Mark in a nutshell—always on the go.

Sean breaks the silence. "Did that help, Bianca?"

Did he kiss me too? No, he didn't. He's reiterating the unanswered question. Maybe this whole thing was too confusing for all of us. Maybe I should have told them that I wanted them instead of anonymously sending them an invitation. That was a spectacularly vague effort on my part.

But two of them are still standing here waiting for my answer, which means it must matter. Surely this time, I can't go any lower. I muster the 'can only go up from here' bravado and meet his gaze.

"Yeah, that's a step in the right direction."

Carl smirks. "A step in the right direction...so Mark wasn't enough."

Oh, shit. Mark's ego would take a hit if they told him he didn't succeed.

"That's not what I meant."

"Help us understand." Sean takes one of my hands, caressing gently. Why does that spark the reminder that I have a thousand invitations to address? That our parents would be horrified to know I lust after my stepbrothers? That I seem to have no purpose in life other than to fail at things.

"It was...just..." I pull my hand back and scramble for a lie so I don't have to admit how much it met every expectation. "Mark's kiss was great...it's just weird since we're related."

Carl reaches for his collar, unfastens his tie, and slides it from his neck. "What if you couldn't see us?"

He moves behind me, positioning it as a blindfold.

Sean's body presses against me from the front. I'm sandwiched between two of my stepbrothers. My entire body throbs with need. How wrong is it to want this?

"I can make you forget a lot more than your ex," Sean leans down to whisper in my ear.

"Can you make me forget we're related?"

His kiss proves he can. I lose track of who's who. A hand brushes up my side. I'm moaning against Sean's mouth. His tongue takes control of our kiss the way I want him to control me. I want to be able to surrender all of my worries.

A hand comes from behind and massages my breasts before trailing down and working its way under my skirt, leaving my panties in place as fingertips slide over my sex. My hips buck shamelessly in response.

The bliss I'm basking in intensifies as he moves his hand faster and faster.

Someone nips my ear. The hand exploring my neck, my back, and my arms has me wondering how many erogenous zones I have.

The sweet nothings destroy my ability to hold back.

"We can make you forget everything. All you have to do is let go. We'll take care of you."

I splinter into a million pieces...to his words, to the mouth on mine, to the fingers working magic between my legs.

When I drift back, my body is no longer braced between them. I'm being carried, set on a chair, and kissed gently.

"Can you come for us again?" Is that Sean?

My head is turned to the side and a mouth is on my neck. The other brother's lips are on mine. The neck kisses trail downward until there's warmth on my sex. I'm lost in blindness.

Why didn't he take my panties off? I fumble to get my skirt out of the way and my panties down.

Carl says, "I guess that's a yes."

Firm hands grip my wrists on either side then swing my hands wide and pin them behind my head.

Warm breath heats my sex—panties still in place. Then the breath is gone. Lips and kisses make their way from one thigh to the other. My hips make their best guess when they can buck into the kisses.

He, whichever brother it is, finally takes pity on me. Pressure on my sex makes me aware of how wet my panties are already. His moans indicate that's a good thing.

"So sweet. I could do this all day." The movement of his lips as he speaks drives me closer to release.

I'm not going to admit that I don't think I could handle 'all day'. It doesn't matter. I'm lost in 'right now' as I fall apart once again.

They take turns making me come. It finally seems like I'm getting something right.

When I wake up, I'm not wearing the blindfold. It's dark. Bodies are on either side of me and I have to wiggle just right to slip out of bed. I manage it without waking anyone.

The faint sound of my alarm filters into my awareness. That's what woke me up. I'm grateful it starts quietly and gets louder. My brothers haven't heard it yet. The faint phone glow from the other room is just enough to help me navigate from the bedroom we ended up in.

I shut the alarm off, and with the little bit of screen light, find my dress and thank my lucky stars that my walk of shame is only to the next penthouse.

As I open the door to leave my brothers' apartment, the elevator dings. I hope that the sound isn't enough to wake the guys, but the door is ripped from my hand.

Mark's standing there. His eyes are bloodshot. He's only in his boxers and his damn happy trail has me salivating. When did he come back? Did he join—

A click from my right draws my attention to my stepmom as she looks up from her phone, shocked.

I follow her horrified gaze to the elevator where Aurora and Cindy are exiting. I didn't realize Cindy was coming too, and I don't have time to celebrate that the invites will go even faster.

"Mark?" My stepmom's comment dictates where all of us look. "What is going on here?"

"I was just...um..." He is rarely speechless, and holds up his shirt, which if my brain can be trusted, he was not holding a few seconds ago. Carl is close behind, grinning. Mom can't see him.

Mark resumes his normal composure. "I dropped this in the hall."

Carl winks at me. "Mark had one of those wild nights. Our lovely stepsister was just returning it."

Their mom motions to me. "Your friends have to go. My invitations won't address themselves. And don't walk into the post office looking like a little Christmas whore."

She turns her ire to Mark. "Why are you still standing there? Cover yourself when there are ladies present even if your sister doesn't know how to dress like one."

Mark and his happy trail step into the lobby. Nerve endings spark to life where his arm brushes mine.

"Don't speak to Bianca that way. The clothes don't make the woman. You—" Mark defends me.

Then he gets yanked backward. I don't know what happened, but their door slams, and I'm left to deal with their mother by myself.

Ten

Carl

I yank Mark by the underwear to get him away from mom. We crash into the wall under his unbalanced weight.

Shoving off of me, he adjusts his boxers. "Bianca was here all night?"

"You would have known if you hadn't run off."

"My head is fucked." He rakes a hand through his hair.

"That's the only explanation for going off on Mom like that. But thanks, man. I was about to defend Bianca. You'll get Mom's wrath instead." I playfully punch his shoulder.

"I'm already going to have to deal with Mom. I want Bianca. I want to get her out of here."

"You have an interesting way of showing it. You should have stuck around and joined us," Sean says from the kitchen.

"You had sex with her?" Last night's level of anger returns.

I answer, "No, but if she needed to forget her ex, I'd say, 'mission accomplished'. She was game for both of us, messing around. What do you guys think about sharing her?"

"How would that work?" I ask, variations of sex acts already vivid in my mind. It's the public life stuff that poses issues I'm not sure any of us are ready to deal with.

Mark finds relative calm. "We should invite her over to discuss what this is."

"She has to address invitations for mom this morning. Carl and I offered to help but she declined. She's going to let us know when she's finished."

I furrow my brow and start to say something but Sean cuts me off.

"Yep, we're at her mercy. Just sit and wait."

I'm not sure what he's up to but after Mark's hissy fit last night, I'm fine with getting petty as fuck and leaving him out of our actual plan. Sean and I arranged to drive Bianca to the post office.

The hours tick by slowly until the moment I've waited for. Invitations are mailed. Her friends are gone. Now the elevator ride back to the penthouse. I watch her in the mirrored wall.

Her smile. Her innocence. Her fun nature. I'm captivated. She's everything this family isn't. And she's exactly what I need. Figuring out how to play this has wreaked havoc on my brain. I can't lose her. I just don't know how to keep her.

For now, we can have fun.

Through her sundress, I cup her ass, giving me a perfect handhold. Why she's wearing a sundress in December is beyond me. She steps to the side and I follow suit until she's pinned against Sean. Her mischievous grin eggs me on the whole time.

I tug at my collar, "Sorry, I didn't put a tie on today."

With the mirrored walls, I can see Bianca from several angles. It's the way it should always be, I should be all-knowing about her. A ding pulls us back to reality. I step away.

The doors open and the fuck if Mom and Mark aren't standing there. Mark is livid. Mom gasps in horror, "What are the three of you...?"

"Just goofing off," I say playfully. Sean pushes Bianca past Mom.

"Your father is coming home around ten this evening. I told him fresh gingerbread would be waiting. I'll be at the spa getting a tune-up before he gets back."

"Yes, ma'am. I'll get some gingerbread made," Bianca says. It takes me a second to process that Bianca understood my mom was telling her to make it. I thought my mom would have it delivered from the bakery. Fuck, she has Bianca under her thumb.

I come to Bianca's defense, "What if she has plans?"

"She can speak for herself. Her father works very hard to afford this lifestyle. And when she goes back to school, he'll pay her tuition. I'm sure she'll be happy to do this small favor for him."

Bianca says, "I love baking. It's no problem."

"Yes, and Bianca already offered to do the baking for the family holiday party since she'll be home."

Mark says, "When is that?"

"The twenty-second." Mom reminds him with a stern look.

He grimaces. "Shit. I think that's when I'm heading to Poland with my friends. They have a stellar holiday light display from what I've heard."

"It would be nice to have you home."

Does Mark hear the sadness in Mom's tone?

She continues, "Please check on that. But more pressing is today's schedule."

I don't want to argue with Mom. I'll let Mark be the bad guy. "We'll make it work."

"Make what work?" Mom asks.

"We asked Bianca to give input on our app since women are our primary demographic."

"I am a woman." Mom juts her chin out.

"Yes, and we'll ask for input from you when we have the app perfected a little more."

Mom beams with pride then quickly turns serious as she points toward the elevator. "That should be fine as long as she has time to bake. And don't let your father see you acting childish like that again."

We all voice agreement.

"And don't forget the homemade—"

Bianca cuts her off, "Whipped cream. I know how he likes it."

I like whipped cream. My dick is hard thinking about Bianca's tongue licking it off of me. I angle myself so mom can't see my reaction. "We better let Bianca get to work, she's got a tight schedule."

"So much to do." Bianca heads toward Mom's penthouse.

Mark asks, "How long will you be gone, Mom?"

Her hand hovers over the elevator buttons. "Why does that matter?"

I can't afford to let Mark's irritation derail us. I answer. "We want to make sure the kitchen's cleaned up."

"I'm going to tea with friends after the spa, I'll be gone until at least eight."

"Great." We all head to the door with Bianca.

Mom's voice pierces the air, "Why are you going with her?"

"Maybe she can teach us a thing or two."

Eleven

Bianca

I breeze through the kitchen, setting the ingredients on the counter. Carl studies me from the doorway.

"What are you doing?"

"Making sure we have everything for gingerbread."

"You don't have your phone or a recipe card."

"I have the recipe in my head."

"Seriously?" Sean asks. "How many times a year do you make gingerbread?"

"Usually just once."

"And you memorized it?"

"Yeah. I love baking. I love taking care of the people around me. Gingerbread's always been one of Dad's favorites. I memorized it long ago. And it looks like we're missing butter."

"That's pretty damn impressive. We've got butter at our place," Carl says. "But what was that mention of homemade whipped cream?"

"Yeah, let's play house." Mark finally pipes up. I wondered how long he would simmer over not being a part of last night. "You better make extra."

"You aren't going to dine and dash like last night, are you?" I tease.

"I had to take care of something."

Sean steps closer and pushes my hair behind my shoulder, planting gentle kisses on my neck.

"I'll be happy to taste test for you." His kisses tickle, and my shoulder hikes up. He winks as he steps back. "And I'm sorry Mom assumes you'll bow to her needs. We'll talk to her. But for now, how much time do you need for the gingerbread?"

"Since I don't need to shop, and I want it to be warm when Dad shows up, I don't need to start for a few hours. Why don't we go work on your app?" I make finger quotes. After all the orgasms they gave me yesterday, it has to be my turn to please them.

Carl pulls out his phone as he laughs. He taps the screen and angles it toward me. "We really do need your help. This is our app."

"Oh." My excitement sinks. "What could I possibly help with?"

"We'll show you."

My heart rate escalates and my panties are drenched as I step into their penthouse.

Carl turns his computer on and a logo similar to the one on his phone populates the screen. He launches into an explanation. It's cute seeing how excited he is.

"When we get this up and running, it will be the top-of-the-line clothing app. We're going to partner with everything from stores that have brick-and-mortar locations to online stores, and even local boutiques like Peaches and Jeans."

"What does it do?"

"You scan your body in, preferably wearing a bathing suit or underwear at most, so the computer can truly assess your shape. When you select clothes you're interested in buying, you can try them on virtually and get the best visualization on the market of how the clothes will fit you specifically. Everywhere from the rise of the jeans to the fit of sleeves. Every detail's been incorporated."

"Ready to get started?" Carl looks at me expectantly.

"Is that your way of asking if I'm ready to get naked?" I can't stop the giggle. For all we did last night, I was blindfolded.

Sean says, "Only if you're comfortable."

This is a good opportunity for the next step. No blindfolds.

Sean notices my hesitation. "If you'd feel better, we could all strip to our skivvies." He's already undressing.

"And we're not even going to make this sexual," Carl says. "I do need to test the app."

It's one of the most ridiculous things I've ever seen—me and my three stepbrothers nearly naked and each of them sporting

55

varying degrees of erections. I grab the edge of the desk to steady myself. It's a lot to go from blindfolds to a lit room.

"Sorry," Carl says, rubbing his hand over the strained front of his underwear. "You're just so fucking beautiful."

How much of a next step will this afternoon be?

"Let's get started." Carl guides me to a greenscreen.

"Unclasp your hands," Carl tugs my fingers.

I have to willingly relent and end up keeping my hands in front of my thighs.

"What's wrong?" Sean asks.

"Just standing here...you can see..." I can't meet any of their eyes, especially Mark's. He's sitting on a barstool nearby. I'm not sure how he'll fit into what Carl, Sean, and I had even though they asked if I'd be fine with including him.

"Are you embarrassed? Sugar, you may have had a blindfold on last night, but we didn't."

Carl cups my shoulders. "Don't slump. Your body is beautiful."

My hands slide up and down my arms. "I'll look better once I lose the weight I put on in college."

"What the hell?" Mark surges toward me.

"As soon as things calm down. I'll go on a diet."

"No. No. No. You don't need a diet," Sean assures me.

"Your mom would disagree."

"She doesn't matter. She overreacts." Mark brushes his thumb over my cheek.

My eyes fall shut. I want to believe him, but it's a fact that I gained weight.

Carl says, "If we haven't proven that we're fine with you just the way you are, let us help you with a few more orgasms."

Mark slides his hand down but I stop it before he gets to my belly.

"You don't have to prove anything. I hear you." But the importance of image has been seared into me far more than a few orgasms can wash away. "Let's do the app."

I swallow my pride and let them document my body from all sides. I'll have them retake the pictures when I lose weight.

Carl moves behind me, circling his arms low on my hips. "It won't affect the way the app puts clothes on your body, but I want the scan to document the way you blush after an orgasm. How about it?"

I close my eyes and lick my lips saying what I'm pretty sure is the right thing to say. "Shouldn't I reciprocate first?"

Sean steps in. "We're not keeping score. You wanted help getting over your ex, we're doing that. You don't owe us anything, although helping with this app would be great."

"I'm pretty sure guys keep score."

"If guys kept score with you, that's their problem."

Heat overtakes my cheeks.

"What's that for?" Mark asks.

"What?" I've probably delayed this as long as I can.

"Why are you blushing?"

"There hasn't been anything to keep score of."

"What?" Carl circles in front of me.

"I haven't had sex, or even an orgasm with a guy... And I don't want to talk about it. Don't make it a thing."

"It is a thing." Mark's possessive expression is back.

"Fine. It's a thing we're not going to talk about. Now let's do the app."

Everyone stares at me, indeed making it a thing. I cringe. Waving my hands, I say, "Shoo. Get your camera. Either we do this or I leave."

They scamper into position around the camera.

We scan my body, they let me select different clothes to virtually try on. It's exciting to see how it works. Then Carl pulls me onto his lap.

"I had a special feature designed. Want to see it?" Nervousness taints his words.

"It sounds ominous."

"Nothing bad, just something you inspired."

"Me?"

Based on Sean and Mark's reactions, I'm not the only one who's confused.

With a few clicks of the mouse, the computer simulates a pregnancy month-by-month. I'm in love with my belly but when my hand goes to my core, it's sadly disappointed. I'm only pregnant on-screen.

"That's amazing." The tears of happiness welling inside of me make it risky to say much more.

Sean says, "I didn't realize you could be even more beautiful."

Mark adds, "Well done, Carl."

"I'm glad you like it, Bianca." Carl dismisses his brothers. "I wasn't sure I'd get to show you."

To be a mom, to have a baby inside of me, that's my dream. But wait. "How did I inspire this?"

"I want to get you pregnant, Bianca."

Surely that's figurative. I'll check Urban Dictionary later for an alternate meaning. His dick is like a rolling pin underneath me. So thick, so hard. I can't focus on the screen anymore. I catch myself rocking my butt over his shaft.

"He's not alone," Sean says. "And I know you want kids."

I croak out, "Yeah."

Mark is a wrecking ball through the beautiful moment. "We can fit them into your career plan."

Thanks for the reality check, bro. "Yeah, lots of women do. Speaking of which, I should go check on my college applications. Alone."

Batting the guys away as I slip my sundress on, I hold back tears. Of course, he thinks I should have a career plan. Of course, they all do. They're all so successful.

Telling them I don't want a career will disappoint them. I need a second to regroup.

Exiting their penthouse, I turn towards my stepmom's. I choke on the memories of her judgment. I don't want to be in this space, in this world where image is everything, where perfection is everything, where success is everything.

Detouring myself to the only space that doesn't reek of them, I cry my way up the stairs to the rooftop.

Twelve

Sean

The click of the stairwell door is a gift letting me know Bianca didn't go check on her college applications. What the hell went wrong?

Sobs come from above. I look up, ready to catch her tears but the door to the roof slams shut. I'm taking the stairs three at a time.

I told Mark and Carl to give me a second with her but they're not likely to listen. I have to hurry. Before I get to the roof, they're following.

Bianca's only a few paces past the door. The brisk winter wind whips past us, reminding me there's a storm blowing in. I wrap my arms around her, first and foremost, making sure she's secure. Her chest heaves against me.

My need to protect her soars to new heights. How can I convince her that she means more to me than any other woman I've dated? I can't even explain it to myself. But if I can't have her, I'll be single and miserable forever.

"I..." If I tell her I love her now, it might seem forced. Damn it. "I hate to see you upset. What's wrong?"

"All of it. We're related...and my school...your business...our parents...just give me space."

I back away. My brothers have stepped on either side of us, and also leave space. Moonlight shines on her wind-kissed cheeks.

Carl says, "We can work this out."

"There's nothing for you to work out. You're already successful. We're in totally different parts of our lives. I'm the one floundering around. I can't even follow my dad's rules correctly: finish high school, get a degree, establish my career. I'm not like all of you."

"Frank's rules...are they what you want?" Carl asks.

"I don't want to throw my life away. There are tons of people who would love to have their college paid for. But it's not what I want...going to college, I mean."

This is huge. Our parents have no idea. I've heard them talk about Bianca's failures, and it irritates me to no end. The only way she's failing is by not pursuing her own path. She's trying to please everyone else. The struggle resonates deeply. I love keeping the peace, but there are limits.

"Being a mother isn't throwing your life away."

"I know that, but they want me to be successful. Like Mark said, I should be fitting kids into my career, which means I need the career first."

"I'm sorry, Bianca. I thought you wanted that." Mark sounds truly sorry.

I shove Mark out of the way. "Success is about knowing what you want so you can strive for it and celebrate when you get there. I'll get you pregnant right now if that's what you want. Fuck what everyone else thinks."

Carl and Mark say something but I'm only listening to Bianca.

The wind catches her dress, blowing it into her face. My cock is rock hard at the sight of her bare legs that wrapped around my head so sinfully last night, and her panties...damn...her virginity. My balls ache with the need to fill her with babies.

She fusses to get her skirt down, but I take it as the universe saying, "Get her clothes out of the way. Time to get her pregnant."

Carl adds logic to the equation. "Hold on. Before we start talking about pregnancy, we should clarify what this is. Mark, are you just in this for fun, or for everything?"

"I'm older than you two. I saw Mom's relationships. They were perfect until they weren't. Commitment changes people. Why can't we play this out slower?"

"He's right," Bianca says.

"There's not a single doubt in my body that I'll do whatever it takes to make you happy, Bianca." I don't need time.

"What do you most want out of life?" she asks me.

"You're not going to let me say, 'pleasing you', are you?"

"No." She's more firm than normal.

I don't understand why she won't relent. Is my brother's indecision the hold up? "What I want doesn't matter. Let's just trust our hearts. What does your heart say, Mark?"

He paces. "Life is bigger than gut reactions. Our parents would disown us. They'd yank the funding from the app. We'd probably get kicked out of the penthouse."

Carl cuts in. "That's all true. So you have to ask yourself, what's more valuable to you, our parents' approval or Bianca's happiness?"

"That's a loaded question. Of course, I want Bianca to be happy. But the three of us can't agree on most shit. How are we supposed to make a relationship with a single woman work?"

Carl offers, "We'll figure it out as we go. I like a plan, probably more than anyone else, but if we wait, we might lose her."

"I don't want to hurt her," Mark calls over his shoulder as he leaves. "I have to make a call."

Bianca points at him. "This is what happens when I'm involved. Everything gets messed up. You guys are arguing because of me and my silly fantasy that we could have something. That you would bid on me at the auction, and we'd end up with a happily ever after."

"Your fantasy?"

"That's why I sent you the invitation."

"You sent that?" Carl says.

She slumps. "I didn't want you to know it was from me. I was afraid you wouldn't come."

"It's always because of you that we'll come. Mark needs time to sort this out. He's afraid of commitment. But if Carl and I can make this work with you, he might warm up."

She gnaws at her lower lip. "I don't want to be the cause of family strife."

"Bianca," I use both of my hands to cup either side of her face and hold her windblown hair out of the way. I have to be sure she's paying attention. "Let me make love to you. Don't worry about Mark or the future or anything. Let me show you how much I love you. And if you want Carl and Mark to be a part of it, I would do that for you. I just want to make you happy."

"At what cost?" Her exasperation crushes my heart.

"There's no cost too high, but I don't want your first time to be up here."

She turns to Carl and her expression shifts, or maybe it's the moonlight glinting in her eye, but I swear something changes. Her shoulders pull back. Her jaw sets. Her eyes meet mine with an intensity she's never hit me with.

"Don't make decisions for me. Everyone keeps talking about me like I'm not here."

"I'm sorry. What do you want?"

"I want to have sex right here, right now."

"Hell yeah." I grab her by the waist and sit her on the ledge, pressing a thigh between her knees, encouraging her to spread for me. Then I lock my lips with hers.

"Thank you for this," I say between kisses.

Thirteen

Bianca

The agony of wanting something that I fear plays out as Sean tenderly kisses me, caresses his hands over my body, and makes room for Carl to join in. The three of us are so perfect, and yet we're still missing a piece.

"You don't have to close your eyes, Bianca."

"I need to." I can't look at them—the men whose hearts I'm going to break. I'm going to fail them like I failed everyone else. I hate that they're so kind and generous. When I dared to look into Sean's eyes earlier, I saw nothing but sincerity. And Carl, there's something between us, like a constant spark. Not just sex but inspiration.

That's how I got this idea.

"How do you want Sean to take you? You're in control."

I don't care as long as we stay up here. I'm free when we're on the roof. I'm enough, or at least Carl and Sean make me feel like I am. But I can't look them in the eyes.

"Let me hop down and bend over."

They stop me before I spin around, each taking their turn caressing my body, tweaking my nipples, kissing my lips, my neck, my arms. They back me against the ledge and Carl drops to his knees. "Can I do this first?"

My eyes shift from his gaze to the gentle brush of his fingers over my shoulder, down my arm to the intertwining of our fingers.

Staring down at him, I understand how much power I have. I'm not used to being in control. Is this what it's like to be surrounded by people who love me for myself?

He unties the sash from my sundress and hands it to Sean. "Let us take away all of your worries. Just exist."

And once again, I'm blindfolded.

Carl grips my waist, trails his hands down my sides, my hips, and wraps his fingers around the backs of my legs. Gusts of wind remind me of my freedom, of my position on top of the world.

"You ready?"

I barely register his question but manage a nod and my cheek brushes against Sean's lips.

Carl's fingers tuck between my legs, pulling my panties to the side, and the wet warmth of his tongue sends jolts of excitement through me. It's different when there are no clothes in the way.

Sean pulls away, and when I reach for him, he takes my hand. A second later he presses it on his bare chest, his heart.

He steps closer, straddling my leg as he presses his body to my side. The thickness of his cock on my side has me more eager than ever to reciprocate.

Carl grips both of my thighs and dives in, eating my pussy like it's the tastiest dish he's ever had. I'm too weak to resist. I give in to gluttony. I'll take as many orgasms as these men will give.

My cream coats his face as I come undone.

"You are the sweetest, Sugar."

A nickname? Why does that feel so intimate?

The heat of his body moves up mine as he stands, his face hovering in front of my blindfold, his warm breath letting me know his lips are poised to let me take in my own scent. I'm consumed by myself, and him, and the rock of Sean's hips.

It doesn't really work to have three people kiss, but Sean tries. He's in on the mix and groans as he licks my release from where Carl's transferred it to my lips. He slides a hand between my legs, slipping easily between my pussy lips, into my center, and another orgasm gathers.

Where are my panties?

"You're so fucking wet. Are you ready for my cock?"

"Yes. Yes, please." Panties not needed.

He spins me to face the ledge, helping me place my hands. Lifting my skirt, he wraps his arms around my hips, continuing to work my clit, driving me to the sweetest surrender I might ever have as his tip nudges at my entrance.

"I'll take it slow. Tell me if I need to stop."

He's respecting the conversation I don't want to have. "I'm ready."

The wind whips past, reminding me the city is laid out at my feet. I don't need my ex. I need my stepbrothers.

There's a sound I can't identify, then Mark's voice. "Have you thought this through?"

Sean's tip pushes a tiny bit farther, spreading my pussy lips. Now is not the time for thinking.

"I know exactly what I want." Sean inches in, stretching me. "She feels better than you can imagine." Sean slides his shaft back and forth in tiny motions.

"I'm here for this. I'm sorry I took so long to get my head clear, Bianca." Footsteps bring Mark closer and he kisses the side of my face.

I cry out as Sean thrusts inside of me. His hands clamp around my hip bones as he freezes. "I'm sorry. I lost control."

"Don't stop. I want that. I want you to mean it."

I didn't know my body could be taken to these heights. So many hands and mouths. I splinter apart over and over again. White heat and stars and rainbows, everything beautiful.

My body contracts around his thick shaft. The surges of tightness, not just from him sliding in and out, but from me reflexively begging him for everything, begging for that baby he said he would give me.

He growls as his cock swells. "If you don't want to be pregnant, tell me now."

I thrust my hips into him. The warmth of his release coats my sex, spills out, and trickles down my thighs. It's a shame any of his seed is wasted. I know what I want—his baby.

I lose track of the other two until Carl speaks up. "You look so fucking hot taking his cock."

"She should take cock more often." Mark agrees.

"She's taking mine next," Carl demands.

Fourteen

Carl

"You're going to have to hold on a second, Mark." I hate to think of it as getting in line, but he can't keep running off and think he deserves time when he returns. Sean and I are invested.

I bend down, kiss Bianca, then move my lips to her ear. "Are you ready for round two? It's a lot for a first time."

"I want it."

I stand her up, facing me, and rub my finger along the edge of the blindfold. "Do you want to take this off?"

"No. It helps me focus."

"Do you want to take this off?" I run a finger down the buttons of her dress.

"I think it better stay on too. You don't need to do anything special."

"Everything I do for you needs to be special."

She smiles nervously and I kiss the tip of her nose, then her forehead.

"I just want to do this with you now while we have the chance."

I'm not sure what to make of her "have the chance" comment. Does she not understand Sean and I are in this? Mark, I still don't know. I can't make heads or tails of where he is with his commitment phobia.

That's not my problem. I turn Bianca's back to me and set her hands on the ledge.

"You ready to let me have a piece of that pussy?"

"Yes."

"We want you to be ours forever."

"You don't have to say that. I want this. Remember, I'm in control of my life. I want to have sex with all three of you."

Why the fuck is she resisting?

"Sugar, we've got you."

"Then prove it."

"Don't fuck this up, Carl," Mark says. Is he worried that she's as commitment-phobic as him?

I glare, grateful Bianca can't see. Then I lift her skirt and admire the glistening streaks of cum running down her legs. I notch my cock at her sopping-wet entrance. Just the tip. I slide in and out.

"You like that?"

"Uh-huh."

"You want more?"

"Yes."

"Then ask me for it."

"What?"

"Ask me for it. Tell me what you want. You're in control of your life."

She hesitates but when I pull away she relents. "I want more."

"More what?"

"I want more of your cock."

I make love to her the way she wants. Later, I'll do it properly.

I don't last much longer than Sean, her release triggers mine. She's that tight, but also, there are three of us and this is her first time. Why is she asking for it to be like this? Blindfolded, turned away, 'have a chance'...is she keeping her distance? Not letting it get personal? Fuck! Are we toys to her?

"Thank you," Bianca says.

I stroke my finger over her cheek. "This isn't the kind of thing you say thank you for."

"Maybe when it's that good, I should."

My cock twitches at her pseudo-compliment, but I have to make one thing clear. "You don't ever have to thank us. It's our job to take care of you."

Fifteen

Mark

Watching Sean and Carl fuck Bianca should give me time to come to my senses. I can't.

I'm wrecked. Her father will pull his company's support for our app, and the dominoes will fall. He's too fucking influential.

But while my brothers were seducing Bianca on the roof, I ran downstairs to make a call to the realtor I've been talking to. I closed the deal on the perfect home in the perfect neighborhood. As soon as I give Bianca the keys, it won't be possible to hide this insane relationship.

I stare at the cum running down her leg and the darkening spot below her where it's pooled. She's so fucking full of cum, and she's about to get a massive load. I'm sure as hell not missing out on my chance to get her pregnant.

"Mind if I taste how divine you are?"

"You'll taste a lot more than just me."

I throw my clothes to the ground as I step behind Bianca. Lowering myself to my knees, I slide my hands up and down her legs.

I can't wait for the feast in front of me. I dive in, settling my lips and tongue on her sex.

Damn, if she isn't worth every bit of risk our relationship poses. I want to be the man for her, to protect her. That's why I bought the house. It's the rashest thing I've ever done. And now that my lips are on her sweet sex, I can't be sure of my motivation.

Am I so hung up on her that I'm still not thinking straight?

Her body spasms, her cries escalate, and she releases with a little squirt on my face. Sweet surrender. She's mine.

When I step back, I drag my hand over my shaft.

Watching her come over and over again for my brothers, I know she regroups pretty damn fast. I slide my cock in.

"I can't believe I can take more."

"I don't want to wear you out. I'll be fast as long as you promise I can take my time later."

"I promise."

My chest swells that she's making promises to me. I hope she'll feel as at home in the house I bought as I feel inside of her.

I piston slowly at first then pick up my pace.

Her cries let me know she's headed from simmer to a full boil, and when she comes undone, she strips me of all my power, all of my ability to protect her because in that moment, I'm reduced to primal need. I have to get my seed inside of her. I thrust hard and fast. I will make her mine even if it ruins me.

Her body stiffens before her release. I take that as my cue to come with her. We're one. We're perfect. She's worth everything.

I wrap one of my arms under her to support her spent body and brace the other against the ledge. "Are you going to let us keep you forever?"

"You're ours, Bianca," Sean adds.

She wiggles out from under me and takes off her blindfold. Sean hands her a shirt to wipe the excess baby batter away.

"Guys, we don't have to pretend this can work. Our parents will never understand."

Carl's head whips from where she's cleaning to her face. "Who cares?"

My blood is boiling. She's right. They'll never understand. Our relationship will cause a rift in the family.

"Get your head out of the clouds, Carl." Bianca's dismissal is a gut punch we all need.

Sean offers, "We don't have to tell anyone right away. Let's take our time. If you are serious about not wanting to go to school, you don't have to. If you want to help with the app, we can teach you things that need to be done, specific skills. Or just let us do it all."

Bianca gnaws on her lower lip. "My dad thinks I don't listen, but I've heard him say it a million times, never mix business with pleasure, and this was definitely pleasure."

She deals such a massive blow, I'm winded.

Sean says, "Then let's keep it as pleasure, but let us keep you."

I find my voice. "We'll lose our biggest investor, but we can deal with that. It's not like we don't have our own—"

Bianca interrupts me. "You did what I asked. You helped me get over my ex. Now, I need to clean up and get the gingerbread going."

Carl steps in front of the stairwell door. "Wait. Did you just use us?"

"You knew what it was from the start. I needed help and you helped me."

"That's not what this was. I love you."

I've never heard Carl speak those three words or sound so hurt. It sucks. It matches how I feel. Glad I'm not the one to put my heart on my sleeve. Except that's a lie. I want to tell her, and I was going to do it with the house. But now?

Bianca's voice is oddly flat. "It's what I want it to be."

How can she be so cold?

She slips past the three of us.

Sixteen

Bianca

I lock the penthouse door. My brothers are still on the roof, no doubt, trying to sort out what just happened.

Pangs of guilt tear at me for pretending I don't care.

I can't stop my reaction to them, but I can stop this madness before it ruins their relationship with my father. It's my first step to being an adult and thinking about someone other than myself.

My next step...move out. I can't always rely on someone to care for me. Their mother has made that clear, and she has the track record to prove it.

While I set all of the ingredients for gingerbread on the counter, I call Aurora.

"I know we have a lot to catch up on, and I promise I'll tell you everything, but I have a huge request."

"What's going on?"

"I need a place to call my own. I was wondering if I could move in with you. I know that's not exactly my own, but I'll pick up another part-time job. I can make enough money to cover half the bills, and rent and whatever else. I need to prove that I can take care of myself for five fucking minutes."

"You know I'm there for you, except I'm not actually there. I'm going to be on the road with my stepbrothers."

"Crap. What have I missed since this morning?"

"We can talk later. You're welcome to crash at my place, and if you can help with the rent, that would be great. When do you want to move in?"

"It won't take long to pack my suitcases. How about tomorrow morning? My dad gets back in town tonight. I'll let the whole family know that I'm moving out."

I add foil cupcake holders to the counter so I can save a few treats for Aurora.

"You don't sound very happy about it."

"It feels like my life's been tossed into a blender. That thing with my stepbrothers exploded, but how can it work?"

"That's a good question."

"It's crazy, right—thinking my fantasy could play out? How can any of us be sure it's real?"

"That's the difficulty of falling in love—ugh, let's table that love word. I've heard it enough times today."

"How many?"

Clunking around from next door tells me the guys came down from the roof.

Aurora sounds as flustered as I am. "Enough to know that it's being tossed around too easily."

"Why is this so hard, Aurora? I just need to prove to myself that I can take care of myself."

"I'll always have your back."

Hanging up with her, I have a sense of pride. I'm going to live the way I want. No more letting my dad use his money to dictate what I do. I have to make this work.

Mentally rechecking the ingredients, I curse at myself.

Butter.

Fuck my life. Swallowing my pride, I head next door to borrow butter.

Their voices hit me in the lobby before I realize their door is open a few inches.

Carl says, "We can make it work."

Mark adds, "Yeah, we lock the deal in. This investment from Frank's company, it's a huge pat on the back. It'll draw in a lot of other investors. We need to capitalize on that."

Sean adds, "We can't lose sight of our priority."

Right, their priorities. It must be nice to have siblings you're close to. They can refocus so quickly.

As I suspected, they were just telling me things they thought a virgin needed to hear. We don't have anything real. They didn't rise to success by letting every pair of spread legs lure them in.

Having heard enough, I knock on their door.

"Hello?" I say sheepishly, pushing the door open. "Can I grab that butter?"

"Hey, yeah." Carl hops off the kitchen counter and heads to the fridge, "How much do you need?"

"Half a stick."

He hands me a full stick. "We told Mom we'd let you teach us. Mind if we come over?"

"You don't have to do that. She won't expect you to learn to cook."

"We could just hang out."

Sean adds, "We can sift the flour or tie your hair back and make sure it's out of the way."

I'm not sure if it's good or bad that they're pretending nothing happened.

Mark says, "And we can forget that awkward post-sex moment. We're all still willing to make sure you're sufficiently over your ex."

A laugh bursts out of me. "We're good?"

"Nothing serious, that's how you want it?" Carl asks.

I nod.

"Then we're good." Carl's response almost seems canned.

Surely it can't be this easy. "Well, I'm going to be making gingerbread." I wave the butter over my shoulder as I walk out. "You're welcome to help, but I have priorities too." Will they catch on that I heard them?

It doesn't much matter because, in seconds, Mark scoops me up, carries me into our parents' penthouse, and sets me on the kitchen counter, "Looks like you've got everything ready."

I like being in his arms way too much.

"I have things to do. I don't just sit around waiting for orgasms all day."

Carl laughs but there might be a note of seriousness. "You could. That option is on the table...or the counter." He drags a hand up my thigh, then grabs a dish towel with both hands, rolls it up, and takes a chip clip out of the drawer.

"What are you doing?"

He places the rolled dish rag in front of my face, holding it at my eyes, and uses the clip to fasten it behind my head. "We need to have a little fun with our chef. Let's play Name That Spice."

His statement is followed by a distinct scent being wafted under my nose.

"Cloves."

"Very good."

Sean seems to be bumping him out of the way, jostling my knee in the process, "And this?"

"Nutmeg."

"You're making it too easy. She had those on the counter." Mark's voice seems to come from the pantry. Seconds later a new scent is offered.

"Rosemary."

"She does know her spices." Mark sounds impressed.

"She also knows that's an herb, not a spice." I join them in talking about me like I'm not there. That gets a hearty laugh from all of them.

Somebody pushes the hem of my skirt up and then traces a finger over my thigh, but it's not just a finger. "Are you rubbing something on me?"

"Can you tell from the texture?" It's still Mark.

"Oil?"

"I thought maybe we could lube you up."

We all know the last thing I need is lube. But they might not know about laundry. "Don't get any on my dress."

"I guess we better take it off."

There's plenty of time. Another romp would be nice now that we're all non-committal. How bizarre has my life become?

Fingers tug at my buttons and soon, they have me standing, they're peeling my dress off.

"This too?" One of them runs a finger under my bra strap.

"Yes."

A finger slides into the waistband of my panties and pauses.

"Yes."

It's easy to say yes when I don't have to look at their faces. Their potential judgment. Deep down, I know I'm thinner than most girls. I know I'm pretty by most standards. I'm just not enough of either of those for my stepmom.

The blindfold keeps me from mistaking a sideways glance as disapproval.

I hear squishy sliding. "How much oil did you put on your hands?"

"How do you know that's what I put on my hands?" Mark asks.

"There are only so many things that make that sound. Hold it under my nose." I wait. "That's canola."

"Damn, you're good, but then again, you already knew that."

I grab his hand while he's letting me sniff the oil and determine that his entire hand is coated. I push it away. "Wash that off."

"It's massage oil."

"I'd need a shower if you coated me with that."

"Oh, dejected." Carl lifts me back onto the counter.

I hear the refrigerator open or is it the freezer? I can't tell.

"How about this?" Sean's fingers touch my collarbone, then ease something cold onto it.

I shiver. "Is that ice?"

"It is."

He trails downward, circling my breast until he makes his way out to my nipple. If I wasn't perky already, I am now. My nipples have to be rock-hard. His mouth latches onto my breast, warming the sensitive skin he just cooled.

"Wow." I tangle my fingers in his hair.

"How about this?" His fingertips touch my knee, then ease the coolness onto my skin, making a slow zigzag toward my sex.

I have goosebumps, and heat is racing through my body all at once.

Closer and closer. Kisses trail up my other thigh until the kisses and ice meet in the middle.

The ice disappears. His warm lips nuzzle my curls. Then he eases the ice cube between his lips, dragging it up and down my slit, "Oh my God, that's so cold."

He pulls away. "Too much? I can warm you up."

"Keep going. I—"

"Holy fuck!" Mark's shock doesn't fit the ice-play thing.

"What the hell?" Who is that? Rustling obscures the voice. I don't know what's happening, but the coldness is gone, and so is the warmth. Everything's gone, even the blindfold gets ripped away.

My eyes squeeze shut against the bright light. The guys are standing in front of me.

"If you were younger, I'd tan your hide."

Oh shit, that's my father's voice. I grab the muffin cups, slap them over my nipples, and clutch my arms over my chest. My dress and other clothes got tossed across the kitchen.

"For Christ's sake, you do realize the glass pan is see-through?" My father is pissed.

Mark shoves the pan to the counter and grabs his pants and my dress.

I want to laugh at the thought of our parents seeing Mark's cock through the pan, but there's nothing funny about this.

"Why didn't you call?" Mark pulls his jeans on and the other two wait for me to get my dress on before they unhand the bag of flour and jar of molasses to get their clothes.

"We didn't know we had to ask for our children to be finished with whatever the hell this is."

Mom says, "Frank got an early flight and I canceled the tea. We texted you but no one responded."

"You boys get out of here. We'll talk later."

The guys each look at me which is sweet, but infuriates Dad. "Now."

"I'll be fine."

With only myself and our parents, Dad says, "Young lady, I thought I was doing you a favor, letting you regroup after flunking out of college, but apparently, this is just pandering to your immaturity. Pack your bags and find somewhere else to stay."

I rush to my room and shove everything in my bags. A text to Aurora confirms it's okay if I head to her place now.

Our parents are in the living room but I don't meet their eyes. I just leave.

Seventeen

Carl

"We get your point," Mark says after Bianca's dad lays into us for a solid twelve minutes without breathing. "We accept full responsibility. We're older. We know better. She didn't force us into anything and we didn't force her into anything. It was a slip in judgment not to use more discretion with what happened."

"Oh, Son, discretion wouldn't solve the problem. You can't fornicate with your stepsister." Mom is beside herself.

Mark's about to blow a gasket.

We had a plan to give Bianca space to keep our relationship fun. We didn't want to force her into something serious even though the three of us brothers are very clear on wanting her. But a key part of the plan was to keep it quiet until she warmed up.

Our parents walking in on us unraveled that plan.

I've tried to play this out several ways in my brain, but despite Frank's lengthy monologue, there's not enough time to come up with a plan that will please everyone. We need a voice of reason.

"Let's look at this logically. We're not blood relatives. No matter how uncomfortable this is, it's no different than any other woman we could've dated."

Frank opens his mouth but I hold my hand up. "I get it. She's our stepsister. That makes it different. But it doesn't change how we feel."

Sean says, "Bianca wants to have room to make her own decisions."

"Damn foolish ones," her father says.

"We're—"

He won't let me continue. "You boys are old enough to think of the practical matters."

"Having the woman we love by our side at work and home seems pretty damn practical." Mark's taking a stand.

"The practical matters I'm referring to are your relationships with your clients. The practical matter of needing clients to buy your app, to support your app, to promote your app. If word gets out that it's run by a bunch of sex-starved, inbred idiots, you'll be the laughing stock. You must always think of your customers."

Mark's and Sean's expressions indicate their patience is wearing as thin as mine. We love Bianca and we'd rather spend time with her than with her father. "We only need *the right* customers."

"And who are those?"

I'm going out on a limb with Mark. "The ones that aren't assholes."

"You may be older than Bianca, but you're still younger than me. You don't understand the way the business world works."

"You don't understand that times are changing, old man." Shit! I might have gone too far.

I rush out, needing to get to Bianca. My mother shrieks something about watching myself, and Frank yells something I tune out. I can't deal with them anymore.

But when I get next door, it's silent.

"Bianca." I'd understand if she yelled at me or was crying. What I'm not prepared for is for her to be gone. Her room is in disarray as if she packed quickly and left.

She was worried she would ruin everything, but she didn't ruin it.

She had an unexpected lesson for us. One we should have handled years ago so she wouldn't be subjected to such scrutiny. Mark, Sean, and I need to become fucking adults. We've got to man up for what we want.

We want Bianca.

Eighteen

Bianca

Hauling myself up the stairs to Aurora's apartment, I'm not sure I'm cut out for working in a diner. I'm merely a messenger passing orders in one direction and plates and cups in another. I'm not doing the fun part of food, the creation, or sharing in the excitement.

But it's a job. It's also less temporary than being Santa's helper at the mall and stocking shelves for last-minute shoppers at the department store. I've been working myself to the bone now that I have to pay my own bills.

I'm almost dead after one week.

Dropping onto the couch, I open my phone. It's safe to do that now that I've blocked my family. I sent them messages letting them know I needed time to myself but my brothers kept calling and messaging anyway. They want to make sure I don't forget about the Christmas dinner. I let them know I'm not going and that they should arrange for someone else to cook.

There's an opening for a nanny in the local jobs listings. That would be perfect. I'd get to try out all of my cooking skills and take care of kids. I rub my belly, remembering how good I looked simulated-pregnant.

My period should start in another day or two. Unless I got pregnant already. I still can't believe how caught up I was in the moment.

My fantasy stepbrother game was strong. Have unprotected sex with all three of them. Everything will be fine.

I'm exhausted. I could use a foot rub.

I try to think if there's any way to mimic one. I toss my phone aside and head to the shower. If the showerhead's cord is long enough, it would work. Anyway, I need to get cleaned up, rest for a couple of hours, and then head to the department store to stock shelves.

The warm water steams up the bathroom before I'm naked and enjoying the warmth running over my body. Grabbing the showerhead, I lean against the shower wall so I can lift my foot, but the enclosure is still cold.

Not a fun kind of cold like the ice cubes.

Using the water to warm the wall, I lean again. It's awkward. I'm tired. I'm pissed that everything reminds me of my brothers.

Letting my foot return to the floor, I drift the showerhead to my sex. An orgasm would be better than a foot massage anyway.

The pulsing water is a distant second or is it a fourth to the guys? My orgasm builds slowly, almost too slowly. I close my eyes, remembering how their hands and mouths felt on me, and their cocks inside of me.

I had to guess sometimes since we used blindfolds, but it seemed Sean's touch was usually the gentlest. Carl was more likely to try to excite me. Then there was Mark. His grip was firmer, more controlling, and that's what kicks my orgasm into gear.

I lean forward, bracing my free hand on the shower wall. I'm almost good enough at pretending to imagine that this mimics the position of the rooftop. My orgasm builds a little faster. It's still not the same. Nothing will be the same as them. I'm probably ruined.

I spread my legs and try to get comfortable. It takes a second to get into it again.

Then the tiniest fireworks show ever erupts inside of me. It's comparable to lighting a single Black Cat after going to the city fireworks display.

Whatever. I finish showering, dry off, and crawl into bed. My drifting-off mind sandwiches me between the guys. I startle awake. They're not there.

In a pathetic attempt at positivity, I remind myself that I'm in control of my life. Yay! It's what I want.

Those heights of pleasure I attained—they give me something to work for. I know how good life can be. My future adult self will get back there someday.

Nineteen

Mark

Elvis's *Blue Christmas* is playing on the PA system at the store where I'm buying decorations. Memories of Mom listening to it over and over again filter into my mind. I thought she just liked Elvis.

Now I get it.

I grab the box of blue ornaments with silver glitter. If Bianca's silence wasn't so deafening, I'd make a blue balls joke when I get home.

My fears that I wouldn't be able to commit, and take care of her, and be enough for her, have come to life. I bought a fucking house and it might as well be empty when I walk in the door and can't say, "Honey, I'm home."

How did I go from the idea of the penthouse being nothing more than a landing pad between trips to buying a house, having a white picket fence installed, and wanting to say that classic line every single day? And that's only when I absolutely can't work from home.

The irony fucks with my head.

Putting up a tree and going through the motions of decorating appease the piece of me that Bianca will realize we're soulmates.

Would things be different if I hadn't held back? If I hadn't let business get in the way? If I'd just admitted that I wanted her instead of pulling that macho big brother shit?

And if we'd revealed our relationship to our parents differently, would they have been less shocked? Yeah, that's a given. There's not a worse way to have let them in on our little secret than by defiling Daddy's little girl on the kitchen counter. The penthouse reeked of bleach for a week with Mom trying to eliminate our sin.

She's doing better now, insisting that we continue with plans for the family's holiday dinner. Mom thinks I canceled my trip to Poland for her. I let her have it.

I won't be leaving the city until I hear from Bianca.

Carl drives us to the penthouse on the day of the party. Snow is starting to gather on the road and the sidewalks have been shoveled.

"Do you think Bianca's going to show?" Sean asks. She's not returning calls or texts.

"Mom hasn't heard from her. And without a car, she'd need a good rideshare driver."

Carl says "I can't blame her for not wanting to face our parents again, that was pretty rough."

"I think she could have dealt with getting caught. But her father kicking her out? Too much." This will be the first time I've seen Frank since *that day*. I promised myself not to throttle him, but I'm popping my knuckles as we ride up the elevator.

The second we're in their apartment, I give a polite hug to Mom, confirm that Bianca isn't there, and storm over to Frank.

"You need to get shit straight with Bianca. We don't know that she's safe. We don't know that she's alive." I pull my voice down. "We love her even if you don't. Give us a fucking chance."

"Whoa, that's a big word."

"Do you need me to define it?"

"I don't know what's wrong with your generation. It's going to hell in a handbasket. All of you think you can share women...your sisters no less. Earlier this week, the social media rag, SmorgasSmut had stories about semi-local rock stars and hockey players sinning with their stepsisters."

"It's not a sin to love someone." My voice is too loud and angry.

Mom pats my arm. "Now, now, Son. Let's be civil."

"I can't be civil when this prick doesn't give a fuck about his daughter."

Frank points to the couch. Sean and Carl sit but I don't budge. A staring contest ensues and I know it doesn't matter who wins. He will in the end. He has seniority.

Sean scoots to the middle, freeing up the end for me. "Come on, man. Let's have a conversation."

So we do. Sean, Carl, and I sit shoulder to shoulder, squeezed onto the couch.

"Don't ever talk to me like that again and don't ever accuse me of not caring about my daughter. I have a tracker on her phone. I know where she goes all day every day, and she is perfectly safe, but she has some lessons to learn and so do you."

"What the fuck?" I jump up.

"Sit down," he yells.

My pent-up energy has me about to explode. I circle behind the couch and grip the back of it to keep myself from punching him. "Where is she?"

"If she wanted you to know, she'd tell you."

"She should be here. It's our Christmas dinner." My irritation borders on petulant child.

Mom defends Dad. "Bianca was included in the group chats. She's choosing not to be here."

"Where the hell is she?"

"Lower your voice, Mark."

"I'm not lowering my voice. You're the scumbag who doesn't value your daughter any more than any other asset. It must perform. It must be perfect. She must be perfect. You two have ruined her."

"Son. She has a lot of growing up to do. She's still a teenager."

"Don't patronize me."

Sean uses his ultra-calm voice, which tells me instantly that he's anything but calm, but he has a knack for this. "Let's focus on Bianca's safety. Can we be sure that she's safe? Does she have people she can talk to?"

"I can assure you she's safe." Frank's assurances don't mean anything to me.

I rush over, yank his phone out of his hands, and toss it to Carl. "Find her."

Carl springs to his feet and is out the door the second the phone hits his hands. He has some computer gadgets in the car. Hopefully enough to get into the phone.

I point at her father. "Don't move."

"You stole my phone."

"Unlike you, I will give up everything for your daughter. Her happiness is the only luxury I can't live without."

"You might want to think about those luxuries before you keep running your mouth. I own this building. I can evict you."

"If you paid more attention, you would have noticed we moved." I storm out, and Sean is only a pace behind me. I yell over my shoulder, "We'll give your phone back when Carl gets what we need."

It's true. Frank has a tracker on her. We can see everywhere she's been. She's busy all day, all night. My poor sweetheart barely has time to sleep. We make note of the address, an apartment complex, then decide to keep Frank's phone in case she leaves before we get there.

Carl offers a piece of wisdom. "We haven't talked about the possibility that Bianca's already carrying one or more of our babies. Now is not the time to point that out to her. Are we clear?"

We agree to focus on getting her back first.

Based on the dot on the phone, we narrow Bianca's location to two possibilities, upstairs or downstairs, of the apartments in front of us.

Aromas of cinnamon and sweets guide me to the upper choice. Her schedule is ragged and yet, she's baking?

As I'm about to knock on the door, a man's voice halts my hand. "I made the biggest mistake of my life letting you go, Bianca. When I set out to find myself, it was because I was young and foolish. I didn't know what I needed."

"I've been doing a lot of self-discovery too. I guess it's what we do at our age."

"I'm sorry I let you go. It turns out that when I looked for myself, I couldn't find me. There is no me without you. Bianca, please forgive me for whatever pain I've caused you." This dude must be her ex.

There's no me without you. That's pretty good, but I won't stand by without a fight. I bang on the door so hard the windows rattle. The whole fucking apartment might shake. We've got to get her out of this place. This isn't the kind of life she deserves.

"Open the door, Bianca."

"Go away. You're supposed to be at the Christmas party," she yells to us.

"Who is it?" he asks.

"My stepbrothers."

Carl angry-whispers, "She told him where she was, but not us."

That's not helping my irritation issues. "Open the door. We're here to take care of you."

The lock on the door clicks but the swing of the door is caught by the chain, after a few inches.

"Let us in, Bianca," I keep my voice low.

"Don't cause a scene."

Sean says, "You belong with us."

Idiot ex has the balls to say, "If she wanted to be with you, she would."

The hair on the back of my neck prickles, and not just because I'm getting covered in snow. If it was possible for me to go into Hulk mode, I'd knock the door down.

Carl says, "Your choice, Bianca... We can have this conversation in front of your ex who foolishly chose to dump you, or we can have it in private."

"Give me a minute."

"Now." I've lost my patience.

"Damon, you better go. We'll talk later."

"I'll stay. I'm here for you, B." Damon doesn't know how close I am to strangling him. His use of a nickname makes it more likely. And when Bianca steps out of sight, the rope holding my restraint in check, frays within a strand of snapping.

"Let him leave peacefully." Bianca eyes us through the slim opening.

A strand of relief fortifies my restraint. I hate to back away even an inch, but I do, and sure enough, she slides the chain off to fully open the door, and her ex, who looks like a decent guy, is standing beside her.

His eyes go wide when he sees the three of us. "Those are your stepbrothers?"

"Yeah."

I swear he shrinks several inches as he tries to slip between us, which is fine.

Bianca ushers us in, and we do our best to shake the snow off rather than track it inside. Keeping us at arm's length, she asks me, "Aren't you supposed to be in Poland."

"I canceled the trip because I was worried about you."

"No need to be so dramatic. I'm fine. Better than ever." Her expression softens.

"Then you didn't show up for the holiday dinner..."

"It was a choice to keep negativity out of my life. I'm sorry it messed up your plans."

"You didn't mess up my plans. I finally found what I've searched the world for...happiness...you."

"Mark—"

He cuts her objection short. "But I didn't protect you. I never thought I'd be the guy to fail his woman. It's the worst feeling ever. I'll never fail you again. Let me take you home."

"I am home." She holds her arms wide. "I can take care of myself. I'm making it on my own. I have multiple jobs. I'm doing my things my way."

"Perfect. Do your things, your way, at the house I bought for you."

She draws back in surprise.

Carl speaks up. "Please give us a chance, Bianca. We stocked the kitchen with all the gadgets the clerk at the store said you could ever need. The only thing missing is you."

"Assuming I'll spend a lot of time slaving over food could be offensive."

"We didn't mean it like that."

"I know." A hint of a smile graces her lips.

I wink. "We got extra soft dish towels."

"Moving in is a big step." She's hesitant but not refusing.

Carl warned us not to mention the possible pregnancy. I'll tread lightly. "Maybe not as big as another step we may have already taken."

Her lips purse almost imperceptibly through a long breath.

Twenty

Sean

We're kind of on probation, but Bianca moved in, so we're headed the right direction. She's ended things with her ex, and her need for personal space gave us time to talk to our parents about how they treat her.

She looks up from her book when I join her on the balcony. Her fingers barely peek out of the blanket she's snuggled in, and hold the page she's on.

Snow falls gently, collecting on the rail. The storm coated the entire mountainside and it glistens in the sun.

I can see why she'd sit out here to read. "I can't decide which is more gorgeous, you or the landscape."

She pats her messy bun. "I warned you. Messy hair, don't care."

The warning is part of her testing if we're truly comfortable with her simply being her. She's so used to being judged, it's hard for her to accept that we love *her*, not the incidentals.

I lean down, kissing the top of her head. "Just kidding. The only reason there are only eight wonders of the world is that you weren't born when they put the list together."

She bats me away. "Now you're just being cheesy."

Arguing wouldn't convince her that I'm being sincere.

She blushes. "Stop staring. Did you come out here just to bother me?"

Oops. It brought out her playful side though so we're good.

"Ready for your first Christmas present?"

"I thought we were swapping gifts tonight. I need five to fifteen minutes to get yours ready."

"That's oddly specific, but your presence is all we need right now."

She snuggles into my chest, her book secure in our bond as I scoop her up.

I set her on a barstool where Mark's laptop is open and the video from our parents is paused on the screen.

The exact moment she sees it, her smile vanishes. Scrambling to shrug the blanket off, she trips and drops her book. We're all there to catch her but she swats us away. The book doesn't fare as well.

It bounces off the counter and crashes to the floor, pages bent.

"I don't want to talk to them. Christmas was going so good."

"Hey," Mark grabs her shoulders. "You're not talking to them. They're talking to you."

"Even worse." She shrugs away, grabbing the book from my hands as I smooth the pages.

Carl catches her arm. "It's a video. They're apologizing."

The ticking of the huge clock on the living room wall counts the passing seconds that count the many ways she was hurt by them.

Did we fuck this up?

She kicks the blanket from around her feet and steps away. I wish I could undo the moment, wrap her back up in the soft pink blanket, and rediscover the sweet smile she had when snuggled against my chest.

Grabbing the blanket from the floor, I return it to her shoulders. "I should have prepared you. We talked to our parents. Did our best to explain how their expectations and judgment hurt you. And that you'll take your own path."

She angles her head up to listen.

Carl adds, "They were surprisingly receptive."

Mark gives her the zinger. "And we told them that if they lose you, they lose us because we've chosen our side."

Tears well in her eyes.

I continue. "They wanted to come over to apologize, but we asked them to respect your space until you're ready. The video was your father's solution. And I truly think you'll like it."

We pile onto the couch, Bianca positioned on Mark's lap, flanked by Carl and me, and we watch the video with her.

Mom spells out the scary and humiliating years when she didn't have enough money to feed us and had to beg friends to let us stay with them. It's why she pushed so hard for Bianca to get a degree. Some of the keeping-up-appearances tie-ins were a little harder to grasp, but she meant well and promises to tone them down.

Frank has a harder time opening up but makes a show of writing a check for the amount he planned on spending on Bianca's education. It's hers to spend however she wants.

Carl keeps the tissues handy for Bianca. I snatch one as I head to the counter. I don't want my brothers giving me shit over a few tears to mar the moment.

"There's one more thing." I grab the envelope our mom sent. Ditching the tissue and resuming my place on the couch, I position the envelope for everyone to read the outside:

To my beautiful (on the inside) children, please open when you are all together.

"She sent this. Who wants to do the honors?"

Carl says, "Bianca should since she sparked this transformation. Are you okay with that?"

When Bianca nods, I set the envelope in her hands. She slides a pink fingernail under the edge of the flap. I hadn't noticed her nail polish matched her pajamas until now.

Finding four pieces of postcard-style stationery, each with one of our names, Bianca hands them out. We quickly determine that Mom has made the same handwritten promise to each of us. She'll always be there for us, no matter the situation, no judgment, no questions asked.

I grab another tissue...so I can blow my nose. I'm not used to this level of emotion in our family. Interesting, everyone seems to do the same.

"That's an incredible gift. I need a minute." Bianca is running out of the room before the words are out of her mouth.

We get our gifts out from under the Christmas tree while she's gone. "What do you think she's doing?"

"By the sounds of her footsteps and the door, I think she went to the bathroom."

"Good thing we didn't follow." Mark cracks himself up. It's good to see him relax. He's finally found the thing he's been searching the planet for, and it was at home.

Bianca does an abrupt halt when she enters the room and we're not on the couch.

"Over here." I wave her gift in the air.

"Your present will be ready in a few minutes." She glances over her shoulder.

"No worries, this isn't your real gift anyway."

"Real gift?"

"This one's sort of utilitarian, and will need a little bit of an explanation."

She takes the package from my hands and unwraps it, holding up two new phones.

"I got you a new phone because yours was a little broken."

"A little? The screen was nearly unusable."

I kiss her nose. "I was being kind."

"And the other phone?"

I take it from her and send a text to all of them. Carl and Mark's phones buzz from nearby but Bianca's is farther away.

"That's my new number. I played it off that night my brothers razzed me about girlfriends, but they were partially right, I had too many *friends*. Now that I have a new number, only the important people can get in touch with me."

"Hearts will be broken." Mark can't resist the opportunity to harass me.

"As long as I never break the one I care about." I pull Bianca onto my lap. We're lost in a kiss when a timer sounds from the other room.

"What's that?" Carl asks, striding to find it.

"Ah! Wait!" Bianca calls. "You all have to get your present at the same time."

"Where?" I ask as she crawls off of me.

"The bathroom."

"Our present's in the bathroom?" Mark stops beside Carl and I join them.

She shrugs.

Carl surges forward first but Mark muscles past him, their shoulders banging into the hallway walls. I'm hot on their heels as we file into the bathroom.

A single pregnancy test stick is on the counter. Mark lifts it. "Fuck yeah!"

A pink plus sign. "We're having a baby!"

Carl says something but I'm running down the hall to wrap our new mama in the biggest hug ever.

Our brothers join us, and too many kisses are swapped to keep track of. Then Carl asks, "How did you know it would be positive?"

"Sore breasts, tiredness, nausea...all the fun."

"This is better than my wildest fantasy. Being a dad feels like I'm king of the world."

While my brothers argue over who the father is, I say to Bianca, "I need to make love to you. Is that okay?"

"If you're worried about having sex while pregnant, I've checked five different websites. They all say it's fine."

"If you want a blindfold, we can use the ribbons off the Christmas tree," Carl says, dragging his fingers over a velvety blue ribbon.

Tangling her fingers with his, she says, "I don't need a blindfold. I want to see it all."

She's giving us gift after gift. I only hope I can make her as happy.

The three of us guys strip then I spread a blanket and pillows over the carpet. Mark eases Bianca onto the pillows and slips the bottoms of her pajamas off. She lifts her arms out of his way as Carl maneuvers her pajama top over her head.

I'm about to take her nipple into my mouth when I remember what she said about the signs of pregnancy. I sprinkle light kisses over her nipples and breasts instead then work my way down to her pussy.

Her curls are soaking wet, glistening with the lights of the Christmas tree.

Mark works his hands over her leg, pulling it wide for me. "You hungry?"

"I'm starved." I settle between her legs and drag a finger through her sex. She tries to suppress a giggle. I ease two fingers inside of her, pump them in and out, and let my thumb brush over her clit with each stroke.

Mark and Carl caress the rest of her body and keep her lips busy. She draws Mark near, licking his shaft like she plucked one of the candy canes off the tree.

My cock hurts too much to draw this out any longer than necessary, so once she has the first orgasm, I lick my fingers, give her a minute to rest, then sink my shaft deep inside of her.

The warmth, the tightness, and her moans, are the best Christmas gifts ever.

Epilogue

Carl

Four years later

The kids are at Aurora's house for the afternoon since Bianca hasn't been feeling well.

Our first pregnancy was triplets and then two years later, we had another baby, and another year out, I'm certain Bianca's pregnant again.

She doesn't think so. She said it's a stomach bug, so I sent her to the doctor. And planned a little fun with my brothers.

We have such a close relationship with the doctor and office staff, that I convinced them to run a pregnancy test with the bloodwork, and only give the pregnancy test results to me.

When the call comes in, Bianca is stretched out on the couch across the room. It's nearly impossible to hide my excitement while she's staring at me curiously.

"Who was that?" she asks when I hang up.

"A business deal. Good things are on the horizon. Why don't you get another nap before Aurora brings the kids back."

"I'm feeling a lot better, but I can squeeze one more in before the circus resumes."

That's the go-ahead I need. I slip out of the room and call our parents. I invite them over for dinner and the plan is in motion. My brother and I want our important people present for our big reveal.

I hear her making a call, and since she has it on speakerphone, I hear that it's the doctor's office. "Your results just came in. The good news is that you're not contagious."

Panic races through me. This could be my only chance to surprise Bianca with a pregnancy reveal. I race into the room as the nurse continues, "Nothing to worry about, just rest."

"That's a relief," I say, playing off my seeming overreaction.

Pulling Bianca's fuzzy pink blanket around her shoulders, I rub her back as she drifts off to sleep.

By the time she wakes up, Aurora is in the backyard with Mark, Sean, the kids, and our parents.

Before Bianca can see any of that, I say, "We have a little surprise for you. Some friends and family are over."

"Why?" She rubs her eyes and looks toward the backyard, but I've closed the blinds.

"You'll find out soon enough."

She runs her fingers through her hair. "I'm a mess. Do I have time to clean up?"

"Trust me. You're perfect." My eyes drop to her tummy, and I'm busted.

Her hands fly to her pajama top. "Is it dirty? I should change."

That was close. "You don't need to change a thing. It's just a few people who love you dearly as you are."

She accepts my hand, letting me guide her to the back door.

"What the heck?" she exclaims when she sees everyone.

My brothers and I are too excited to delay the reveal.

I spin her around, sit her on top of the cooler, and kneel in front of her.

"What are you doing?"

"Something that we should have done a long time ago. Bianca, I kept wanting to make this right and perfect and I kept letting you talk me out of it while you said you needed to get your life in order. But look at everything you've created."

I motion around us, and we have everyone's attention at this point.

"You've made these beautiful babies. You've brought our family closer than ever, and you've provided the most welcoming home for my brothers and our children.

I don't have to worry about my mom taking offense. We've talked to her about how much we value everything she did for us.

113

"Bianca Sinclair, will you do me the honor of fulfilling the most important contract, the most important investment, the most important alliance of my entire life, and marry me?"

Sean steps next to me and kneels. He drags his hands up and down her bare leg. "I hope you'll do me the honor of allowing me to be a part of this crazy endeavor and marry me too because I can't imagine a life without you."

Mark kneels on the other side but bumps me a little so he can get slightly more to the center.

"Bianca, no one's ever challenged me the way you have. No one's ever made me lose control and like it. No one's ever made me so happy to settle down. You make me feel completely insane. But I can assure you, it's of sound mind that I too want to marry you. And I hope you'll take all three of us as a package deal because, well, let's face it, visitation rights are going to get complicated if you don't."

"Oh my gosh. Yes to all of you!"

Tears well in her eyes, and her hands cover her mouth while we embrace her.

Mom steps up beside us, cutting into the moment. "I don't mean to pry, but do any of you have a ring?"

"We planned this in a hurry, but we'll get rings, Mom."

"A hurry?" Bianca's brow furrows.

"It's the other surprise that's the ticking clock," Carl explains.

"Another surprise?"

"You're pregnant."

And we live happily ever after!

Would you like a little more **Baking and Blindfolds**?

If you'd like to go for an elevator ride with these naughty stepsiblings, grab this BONUS SCENE by signing up for my newsletter.

Once you subscribe, I'll keep you up to date on my stories, sales, and other Super Hot content you won't want to miss!

Visit my website: https://SylvieHaas.com

And true to my initials, SHhhh, I'll let it be our little secret.

More from Sylvie Haas

Up next in the Christmas Cherry Auction is **Carols and Consent!**

https://mybook.to/CCACC

———ell———

Eggplant Canyon Phase 2: The Bratva Moves In

This series is full of Book Boyfriends, Bulges, and Bratva!

https://mybook.to/EC2Bratva

More completed series...Come hang out in the original Eggplant Canyon!

https://mybook.to/EggplantCanyon

If you don't like having to choose 'just one' when it comes to donuts or men, you better submit an application for Sugar D's Speed Dating!

https://mybook.to/SugarDsSpeedDating

Grab a seat at the Christmas ~~Cheer~~ Cherry Auction:

https://mybook.to/ChristmasCherryAuction

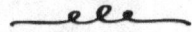

Or check it all out at:

https://SylvieHaas.com

Sylvie Haas
Freebies

Do you love bonus content?

Sign up for my newsletter and you'll get access to all of my freebies, and I'll keep you up to date on all of my new releases and special offers.

https://SylvieHaas.com

About the Author

Sylvie Haas obsesses over dirty-talking heroes who fall hard and fast for the woman of their dreams. And you'll find multiple heroes in one book because she has such a hard time making the heroine choose one possessive guy.

On most days, you can find Sylvie with the wind in her hair, her fingers on the keyboard, and her mind in the gutter as she thinks up new places her characters can get frisky.

Sylvie's books will always deliver a happily ever after, and even though they're short, they'll leave you satisfied!

If you haven't signed up for her newsletter yet, there's still room. The more the merrier!

https://SylvieHaas.com